"What is y̶o̶ ̶ ̶ ̶ ̶ Miss Linley?"

Andrew reached over and lifted her hand, examining the palm as he spoke.

"Were you orphaned, perhaps?" he asked gently.

Meg seized the opportunity to tell the truth. "My father died when I was young," she admitted, "and my mother has fallen on hard times. There is a younger sister, whom I dearly love and hope to see well married."

"But what of yourself?" he asked, still holding her hand. "You are quite fetching, my dear, if you will forgive my boldness. I cannot imagine why you should have taken this post so far from town."

Plucking up her courage, she said, "Nor can I. It was not precisely a decision so much as a . . . an accident, my lord."

"You mean to spin me that story again," he teased.

"Yes," Meg whispered. "I had meant to tell you . . ."

His lips grazed hers, ever so softly. "Forgive the liberty, Miss Linley," he murmured. "But I daresay we have more important things to discuss."

Any objection Meg thought of making flew out of her head as he kissed her again.

A LADY'S POINT OF VIEW

JACQUELINE DIAMOND

Harlequin Books

TORONTO • NEW YORK • LONDON
AMSTERDAM • PARIS • SYDNEY • HAMBURG
STOCKHOLM • ATHENS • TOKYO • MILAN

For Fern Breslow Seltzer

Published November 1989

ISBN 0-373-31114-1

CHAPTER ONE

Miss Margaret Linley was variously known as "high in the instep," a "dull piece of business," and a "great gawk." None of these terms was meant to be flattering, despite her passingly fair figure, soft brown hair, and large blue eyes. For if she was not slighting a gentleman altogether by her inability to see him properly, she was tripping over his boots or ignoring his conversation in her attempts to avoid collisions.

On this particular night the young lady, in her second season and garbed in cherry-red silk, stood holding a glass of lemonade in her gloved hand and trying not to squint. The month was May, the evening was Wednesday, and the place, as any of London's elite could not have failed to discern, was the fashionable if plain assembly rooms known as Almack's, in King Street.

Through the tapestry of the gathering were woven gentlemen in finely cut coats in subdued colours as decreed by the master of style, Beau Brummell. Ladies, each the proud possessor of a voucher which permitted her entry to the premises, danced and laughed and flirted behind painted fans, displaying an almost shocking amount of bosom above their lace-trimmed, embroidered gowns. Those in their first season wore white, while their older sisters displayed themselves in lilac, apricot, peach, and primrose.

The anxious mamas formed a dark border of blues, greens, and purples as they hovered about the dance floor, each hoping her daughter made a fine match. The assemblage overall presented a fabric of such rich colours that Meg, who could perceive little beyond the bright tones themselves, was delighted.

Several ladies strolled by, nodding politely, and Meg nodded and smiled back. But when the ladies turned away without speaking, she wondered if she had mistaken head shakes for nods.

She felt exceedingly uncomfortable. Her mother, Lady Mary, had insisted on dampening her petticoats to make the gown cling to her slender form, and Meg wished fervently that she might change into the old, modest bombazine she wore about the house. Dampened petticoats might be alluring, but they felt deucedly clammy.

Meg's musings halted as a figure in black approached and asked for a dance. She agreed with some enthusiasm until, after setting aside her lemonade, she recognized her partner as a confirmed old bachelor who had no doubt made the offer out of respect for her late father.

Walking across the floor took far more courage than one might suspect, for the whole of the room posed a giant blur for Meg. She attempted to move forward with grace, dreading one of the hideous stumbles which plagued her life.

She must keep her weakness of vision a secret. No one, so Lady Mary insisted, would marry a chit who at nineteen already required a lorgnette, although Meg suspected this was more a fancy of her mother's than a dictum of society. Still, Lady Mary was not a figure her daughter cared to cross, even when, with the unconscious arrogance of one who could spot a paste jewel or hennaed hair across a ballroom, Meg's mother insisted that anyone could see well with a bit of effort.

She refused to permit her daughter a quizzing glass, and had it not been for the generosity of the nearsighted house-keeper, Mrs. Pickney, who was willing to share her eye-glasses, Meg's needlework would have been speckled with blood from her pricked fingers, much the way her life in society thus far had been blotched by her bumblings.

"Are you enjoying the season, Miss Linley?" her partner asked as he guided her awkwardly through an approximation of the waltz, that daring new dance which permitted a man and a woman an almost indecent amount of intimacy.

"Indeed." She gave a silent prayer of thanks for this new dance, however it might distress her elders. With a man's hand on her waist and the other palm-to-palm with her own, she felt far safer than trying to navigate unaided through the intricacies of a quadrille.

"Have you not a sister in town this season?" the man continued. For the life of her, Meg could not recall his name.

"Yes, Angela." Meg bit her lip as her heel brushed the ankle of another whirling young lady and won her a reproving glare. "She's but eighteen months younger than I." Being halfway through one's second season and still unmarried was not yet cause for alarm, but neither did one wish to appear any older than one was.

"Is she here?" he asked.

"Oh, no, she's not yet out," Meg said.

"Not out? Then surely her ball must be due soon, and I've not seen an invitation," the fellow complained. Mr. Crotchety, she decided. That name would do as well as any.

"It's not set," she admitted. "Angela turned eighteen only last week, and it may be she won't enter society until next spring."

Mr. Crotchety seized upon this statement to elaborate at length on the desirability of ladies marrying early and the foolhardiness of keeping them in the schoolroom past the age of sixteen. Meg was tempted to ask him why he felt so strongly about the subject as he showed no predilection for the female sex at any age, but she managed to refrain.

Privately she agreed that Angela should be brought out this year, but debuts into society were expensive. The painful truth was that the Linleys could not afford it.

Tony Linley had been the eldest son of a viscount, and Lady Mary the daughter of an earl. Who could have foreseen that he would die in a carriage accident before succeeding to the title, and who would have guessed that his widow would be left with only a small pension and the remainder of her dowry?

The family fortunes might yet be saved if Meg were to make a wealthy match, but young men with full purses had a way of preferring ladies of substantial means. Moreover, Meg did not think she could bear a loveless marriage, perhaps to some old man such as Mr. Crotchety, with his cracked voice and onion-laden breath.

For herself, she would not have minded suffering through half a dozen seasons without a husband, but Lady Mary could not afford to have two daughters out in society at the same time. The cost of gowns alone was prohibitive, and until Meg married or retired from the field, her flaxenhaired and much more comely—to Meg's mind, as well as her mama's—younger sister must wait at home.

"Meg!" The music had scarcely ended when Helen Cockerell was at her side, pulling her away from Mr. Crotchety. "I haven't seen you all night."

"And I most certainly haven't seen you," Meg returned with a laugh, for her friend was privy to her closest secrets.

"Wait until you hear..." Helen possessed a talent for gathering the latest on-dits like spring flowers in a bouquet. As the two girls adjourned to the refreshment table for lemonade, Helen kept one arm linked helpfully through Meg's and her tongue buzzing with gossip of engagements, fallings-out, and scandals of every sort, all of which she relayed without a trace of malice.

As they strolled, Meg kept a vague smile playing about her lips, for she dreaded giving offence and knew that she often did so by failing to see a gesture of greeting.

"There is Lady Jersey, nodding to you," murmured Helen, and Meg bowed her head politely. One dared not antagonize the patronesses of Almack's. They held the power to deny one a voucher, a punishment which meant exile from the cream of London's ton.

"Now here is my favourite titbit," Helen continued. "Do you recall my cousin, Germaine Geraint? The Friday-faced chit who liked to race her carriage in Hyde Park?"

"No, but she sounds enchanting," Meg teased, nibbling at a bit of stale cake. Almack's was noted for its poor refreshments.

The response failed to make a dent in Helen's monologue. "No, of course you wouldn't, but she had a season seven years ago, for she is five and twenty now, and created such a scandal with her carryings-on that she was sent away to rusticate." She paused for dramatic effect. "Well, she has a suitor!"

This bit of news did little to excite Meg, who had never met the lady in question. "How fortunate for her."

"But you haven't heard who it is!" Helen cried. "Lord Bryn!"

The marquis was known to Meg by reputation, for he often figured in the general gossip. Formerly a rake and a hell-raiser, he had changed considerably after joining Wellington's forces on the Peninsula and suffering a gunshot wound to the leg.

The injury had left him with a limp. Furthermore, the gossips had faithfully reported, he declared upon returning to London that after what he had seen on the battlefield he had no patience with the empty frivolity and wasteful excesses of the fashionables. With that, his lordship had retired to his country home near Stockport in Cheshire, where he lived with his orphaned niece and nephew and had for the past two years ignored the world in general.

"I've heard that he's quite handsome," said Meg, who could rarely tell for herself whether a gentleman was attractive. "Why should he court your cousin, if she's as plain as you say?"

Helen shrugged. "Needs an heir, I daresay. Besides, Germaine's a great gun in her own way."

A gentleman appeared at Miss Cockerell's elbow, claiming the next dance, and Meg watched regretfully as her friend departed. In the battlefield which masqueraded as the social season, it was rare to find an ally, she reflected as Lady Mary bore down on her.

The widow wore a black dress which she often complained was frayed around the edges, although Meg was unable to determine if indeed this was so. A small silver turban sporting a single ostrich feather topped Lady Mary's elegant head.

"Let me see your dance card," she commanded, and Meg handed it over reluctantly. "What? But this is blank!"

"Mother," she said, "I've been giving the matter some thought. Perhaps it would be best if I left London for the season and gave Angela a chance. If she were to make an advantageous match, it might help me, as well."

"Nonsense!" Lady Mary handed the offending card back to her daughter. "The first must be married before the second, unless she is unmarriageable, of course. And you are not."

"But why?" Meg protested. "I don't mind. I like Derby, and even though the cottage is rented to our cousins, surely the Barkers could spare me an attic room."

"Hush!" Her mother stared about them to see if anyone had overheard. "You have more hair than brains, girl!"

A rotund fellow stumbled against them, alcohol shading his breath during his stammered apology. Lady Mary pretended to misunderstand. "Why, of course you may dance with my daughter, Sir Manfred," she proclaimed, and stepped aside. There was nothing for either of the two unhappy young people but to comply, and so Meg bounced her way through a country dance in uncomfortable silence.

Toward the end of the dance, she heard voices calling out and a general stir from afar and concluded that someone of note had arrived. It was nearly eleven o'clock, after which time even the Prince Regent himself would be denied entrance.

Meg glanced toward the doorway, but as usual could make out only indistinct forms. She blushed, remembering one humiliating occasion on which she had crossed a room in full public view only to find herself greeting a valet.

The music ended with a flourish. "Thank you, ma'am," said her partner, sweeping into a bow. Meg bobbed a small curtsey, to discover when she lifted her head that Sir Manfred had vanished, leaving her stranded in the midst of assorted bodies which were already forming sets for a Scottish reel.

If only Helen would appear! But there was no sign of her. With a sigh, Meg lifted her skirts and stepped carefully across the dance floor. She must make her way to safety on her own this time.

Using great care, she approached the haven of the sidelines. As Meg well knew, it would be impossible to concentrate on her path if she watched those around her, and so she could only hope that no one was nodding a salutation.

Where was Lady Mary? Meg lifted her head for a moment, seeking her mother's aid without success. But even if her parent had been watching, she might have refrained from helping her daughter in the belief that, under duress, Meg would suddenly acquire the necessary vision.

With an exhalation of relief, Meg stepped past the last of the couples now contorting on the dance floor. Vaguely she noted a cluster of gentlemen ahead and swerved to make her way around them.

A collective gasp of horror from these same gentlemen was her first clue that she had committed a major faux pas. Meg turned abruptly, hoping against hope that whatever had occasioned this outpouring of shock had nothing to do with her.

She was, unfortunately, quite mistaken. The assemblage broke into fluttering fans and gossiping voices which lingered over such phrases as "I never!" and "The brass of that girl!" And worst of all, from a massive woman with a voice like a trumpet, "I daresay there will be no more vouchers for that miss, or her family!"

At last Lady Mary approached. "What have I done?" Meg pleaded, near tears.

Her mother stared at her reproachfully. "You have cut Mr. Brummell! He nodded to you and you swept by without so much as a word."

"But I didn't see him!" Meg protested. "I was too busy trying not to bump into anyone! I shall go back and apologize."

"Too late." It was Helen, joining them even at risk of bringing scandal upon herself. "He has gone off in a temper."

There was nothing more to say and nothing more to do save gathering their pelisses and walking with bowed heads through the throng. Meg knew her disgrace was complete. Everyone would say she had always been arrogant, slighting even her closest acquaintances, and finally she had gone too far.

Meg and Lady Mary forced their way through the crush of carriages until they reached their own faded barouche, taking refuge within on the velvet squabs.

"I don't know what we shall do," cried Lady Mary once they were under way. "We are ruined. There will be no more vouchers for you or for Angela now."

Her own shame Meg could bear well enough, but it hurt her beyond measure to have done harm to her sister. "Perhaps all is not lost," she said. "I could send round a note of apology to Mr. Brummell in the morning, explaining about my weak eyesight."

"Then you will be the laughingstock of the town!" lamented her parent. "That is scarcely better."

"Well, I shall write a note to say I did not see him," Meg said in discouragement, for she realized that a mere letter could never atone for creating a public spectacle.

"No one will believe it, for he was directly in front of you, but perhaps he will spare us the worst of his anger," Lady Mary said. "Still, had I not already rented the cottage to the Barkers, I should consider packing up the three of us posthaste...." The older woman's voice trailed off with an unaccustomed tremor.

Leaving London would greatly distress Angela, Meg knew, for the younger girl had looked forward so eagerly to entering society this season. And where was the guarantee, once they departed, that next year they could afford to return at all?

The time had come to renew her earlier suggestion, Meg decided as the carriage rattled through the dark streets. "I shall go back to Derby alone, after penning my apologies to Mr. Brummell and the patronesses. Under the circumstances, surely no one will condemn Angela for my actions. We might even be spared the expense of a ball, and Angela can come out quietly at a tea party. Everyone will think we are acting with discretion."

Lady Mary frowned as she considered this notion. Indeed, she deeply loved her elder daughter and would not willingly see her banished, but it did seem the most expeditious solution.

Angela was not so restrained when they arrived home and told her of the night's catastrophe and their contemplated course of action.

"You cannot!" she told Meg. "How can you go to live with our cousins? The Barkers are a pair of old grumbletonians. They'll stuff your ears with *Fordyce's Sermons* until you run screaming down the street!"

"I'll never run screaming down the street," said Meg. "I would collide with a milk cart."

"You're not so bad as that!" objected Angela loyally.

"To your beds," said their weary mother. "We'll discuss this in the morning."

Seeing the sleepiness of the little maid, Karen, who attended them in addition to her other duties, the girls sent her off with assurances that they could make their own toilet. As she allowed her sister to brush out her hair, Meg reflected that what she would miss most was not the balls or outings to Vauxhall Gardens or boxes at the Opera, but her family's companionship.

"Is it truly so difficult for you to see?" Angela asked, gently untangling a knot in Meg's curly locks.

"Yes. In spite of what Mother says, I can't simply force my eyes to function properly." Meg toyed with a pink velvet ribbon on the dressing table. "If only she didn't insist it's so shocking to be seen with a lorgnette."

"I can't imagine what good it would do," said Angela. "I looked through Mrs. Pickney's glass once and it gave me the most frightful headache."

Impossible to explain to someone with good vision how a tiny bit of glass could open up an entirely new world, a realm of sharp edges in place of fuzzy ones, where furniture and faces no longer faded to obscurity within half a dozen feet, Meg mused as she climbed into bed.

Despite the silence that fell over the premises, there was little sleeping done that night in the Linley household.

In the servants' quarters, the coachman spread the gossip he had overheard about the evening's mishap. In addition to their distress at Miss Linley's fall from grace, the staff worried that Lady Mary might retreat from London, leaving most of them to seek out new positions.

The maid, Karen, lay awake for a different reason, one sufficient to overcome her exhaustion. She was concerned not for her mistresses—what real harm could befall members of the nobility?—but for how she might reach her childhood sweetheart, Peter, a valet who worked in Liverpool. His master intended journeying to Canada, and Peter had written to beg that she come and marry him so that they might go together. But how was she to get north by herself?

One storey below, Angela also lay sleepless, hurting for her sister and trying not to dwell on her own disappointment. How her young heart had swelled, the times she was allowed to accompany her family to Vauxhall or Hyde Park and handsome men doffed their hats to her. Would she never dance in the arms of one of them?

Lying beside Angela—for the sisters shared a bed—Meg longed heartily to be done with the whole business. She could bear even the Barkers' endless sermonizing; at least she need not fear that the least misstep would lead to disgrace. Perhaps in Derby she might even acquire a quizzing glass.

As for Lady Mary, she had a difficult decision to make. Since her husband's death, she had been forced into a situation for which her gentle birth and upbringing had never prepared her. At each turning point, she discovered with amazement new sources of strength within herself.

So it must be now. Only she knew the truly threadbare state of the family finances. She had refrained from telling even her eldest daughter, but there would be no season the next year for either of the girls unless one of them found a wealthy husband this summer.

It was only sensible that Angela be given a chance. As Meg said, after a written apology and the offender's retirement from London, the ton would soon forget this tempest in a teacup. And within a few weeks, Angela might take her place in society.

Meg would rub on well enough with the Barkers, Lady Mary reflected, and if Angela made a good match, it would pave the way for Meg's return to society next year. It was the best one could hope for under the circumstances.

CHAPTER TWO

THERE WAS NO QUESTION of making calls the following afternoon, for the Linleys knew that no one would be at home to them.

"It's monstrous!" cried Angela as the three of them sat in the parlour in funereal gloom. "I don't want to be accepted by the ton if they're so cruel and petty, Mother. Why don't we all leave?"

"That wouldn't serve," her parent responded coldly. "We'll hear no more talk of that sort, miss."

Angela turned to Meg for help, but her older sister shook her head. "It's for the best," she said. "I shall be just as happy in Derby as here, save that I'll miss my family. One and a half seasons of Venetian breakfasts and card parties are enough for me."

At that moment, the three were surprised to hear a carriage stopping outside in the street. Angela would have run to the window but for her mother's restraining hand. "You might be seen, dear," cautioned Lady Mary.

When the butler entered a moment later to announce Helen Cockerell, the sisters were delighted.

"Oh, Helen, I knew you wouldn't desert us!" Angela sprang up to greet the older girl.

After the usual fuss of settling into place and pouring tea, the Linleys took turns informing Miss Cockerell of Meg's impending departure from London. "I sent round the note to Mr. Brummell this morning," Meg concluded. "There was no response, but I hardly expected one."

"Oh, that fop!" With a wave of the hand, Helen dismissed the second-most powerful man in London, at least so far as the social lives of its younger set were concerned. "There's talk that he's given offence to Prinny more than once, and there'll be a falling-out before this time next year, you mark my words."

Everyone knew that Brummell's success depended on his close friendship with the Prince of Wales, who had become Regent in February. That Brummell might fall from grace hadn't occurred to Meg, but in any event it was sure to come too late to help her.

Angela was more optimistic, her blue eyes widening. "Then perhaps Meg might stay—"

"I think not," said Lady Mary.

Reluctantly Helen concurred. "For myself, I shall miss her terribly, and write every day. But even my own brother, Edward, confesses himself horrified at Meg's conduct—you know what a stiff cheese he is! I've no doubt he'd have forbidden even my coming today if he'd known of it."

Edward, being a good ten years older than his sister, had become her guardian after their parents' death. Despite his fair colouring and generally admired appearance, Meg regarded him as little warmer than a block of ice. Stiff cheese indeed!

The sisters bade a tearful farewell to Helen, who embraced Meg lovingly and renewed her promise to correspond faithfully.

Welcome though it had been, the visit left behind an even gloomier atmosphere than before, as if the last hope were removed.

It was decided that Meg should take the mail coach to Manchester. Although that meant journeying a bit beyond her destination and paying a stiff fee, the journey could be accomplished in eighteen hours instead of several days, thus saving the expense of rooms in posting houses. From there, she and Karen, who was to accompany her, would hire a post chaise to Derby.

On Friday, Meg sorted carefully through her gowns, choosing those of darker colours and more severe styles. She selected practical fabrics—kerseymere and chintz, bombazine and calico.

"There's no need to go about looking like a spinster!" Angela protested when she entered and saw the dresses her sister had laid out.

"Don't be nonsensical," said Meg, returning a gown of pink crepe to the wardrobe. "What would I do with these fripperies in Derby? The Barkers would prate of sinful dress until my head ached." For, as fashion decreed, the gowns displayed an unseemly amount of bosom and clung to the figure, even when not dampened.

Angela laughed. "Well, I certainly can't wear them. I'm half a stone lighter than you and two inches shorter."

But they would have to be made over to fit Angela, though Meg saw no point in telling her sister now. Perhaps Lady Mary could find the funds for a few new dresses; otherwise Angela would certainly be disappointed.

"I believe I've picked out the appropriate clothing," Meg said as she selected matching gloves, shoes, shawls, ribbons, reticules, cloaks and pelisses.

After Angela departed, Meg ticked off on her fingers the tasks which had been accomplished. She had written her apology to Mr. Brummell, Lady Mary had dashed off a note to the Barkers regarding the impending arrival, the clothes had been selected.... Ah, yes, her books!

A short while later, Meg was returning to her chamber with an armload of her favourite novels and poetry when she encountered Karen in the hall. "Please, miss, may I speak with you privately?" the girl asked.

"Why, yes, of course." Puzzled, Meg entered the room. Could it be that Karen objected to travelling back with her?

Possibly the girl had acquired a suitor here in London. But Meg vaguely recalled that Karen was betrothed to a young man in Derby. Or had he moved from there with his employer a year or so past?

The maid cleared her throat and stood with her hands in back of her, trying to work up the courage to speak.

"Come now, Karen, we've known each other for years," said Meg. "You've no need to be afraid."

"Well, miss—" the girl peered at her anxiously "—it's this way. My beau, Peter, he's been working in Liverpool."

"Yes?" Meg tried to sound encouraging.

"His master's sailing to Canada in two weeks' time, and Peter must go with him, for there's no other work to be had." Karen uttered the words in one gusty breath. "He wants to marry me and take me along."

"I see." Meg sank into a chair. "You've waited until the last minute to take your leave of us, Karen."

"I didn't see how I was to get there," the maid pressed on, her tongue loosened at last. "I haven't enough blunt, and neither has he. So I thought all was lost, but now I've enough to get from Manchester to Liverpool, begging your pardon, miss."

Meg began to understand. "So you want to leave me in Manchester to make the last stage of my journey alone?"

"Oh, please, miss." Karen looked as if she might kneel to make her plea, an alarming prospect to Meg. "I know it's a disloyal thought. A young lady like yourself mustn't travel alone. But I thought, well, if I hired the post chaise in Manchester for you, what harm could befall you twixt there and Derby?"

What harm indeed, Meg reflected. The ton would be scandalized by such goings-on, but they need never know of it. As for the Barkers, they would object to almost anything she did; there was no pleasing folk with such starched-up notions.

She couldn't recall Peter clearly, but she could see how Karen's face shone when she spoke of him. Why should a girl be deprived of a lifetime of happiness merely because she lacked coach fare between London and Liverpool?

"Very well," Meg said. "But you must say nothing of this to anyone. Not to anyone, do you hear? If Mother learns of it, she'll send another maid with me."

"Oh, thank you, miss." Karen caught up Meg's hands in hers and, to the older girl's embarrassment, kissed them eagerly. "I don't know how to thank you!"

"Just be sure you hire the post chaise before you depart," Meg said. "With my weak eyes, I could never manage for myself."

"Indeed I shall!"

Footsteps approached in the hall, and Karen busied herself with the ribbons on the dressing table as Angela entered.

So the days passed until Monday, when Meg was to depart.

CHAPTER THREE

MEG HUGGED her sister and her mother twice each, ignoring the indifferent jostling of the crowd in the inn's yard. "I shall write as soon as I arrive," she promised. "You must answer at once, and tell me about Angela's come-out. I am certain she'll have a great success!"

"We would be happy with a modest one," said Lady Mary. "At least we may count on the support of Miss Cockerell, and her family is well placed."

"We're to go to Vauxhall tomorrow night, have I told you?" cried Angela, who had informed her sister of that fact no less than three times. "Perhaps I'll meet a handsome stranger!"

"You must speak to no one unless you've been introduced." Meg hoped her high-spirited sister wouldn't create her own scandal. "Don't go wandering away from Mother. Vauxhall's full of footpads and murderers and worse."

"What could be worse?" asked Angela as their groom handed a trunk to the coachman.

"Never mind," replied Meg with the condescension of one who has been out in the world, although in truth she knew little of what "ravishment" meant save that it ruined one's reputation permanently.

Their conversation was interrupted as the mail guard, splendid in a coat of scarlet with blue lapels and white ruffles, lifted a curved bugle to his lips and sounded forth a stream of notes the like of which Meg had never heard before. She suspected he had composed the music himself.

"We're off, then," she said, giving Angela's hand a final squeeze and trying to ignore the lump in her own throat. "It won't be so many months before we're together again. And then I hope we shall be planning your wedding, dearest."

Aided by the many-caped coachman, she stepped into the smart maroon-and-black coach. She ignored the half-dozen riders who gazed down from their perches on the roof, except to wonder how they would keep from being thrown off when the carriage hit a pothole.

Karen was already within, awaiting her mistress. Their companions for the journey were a solidly built merchant and his wife, and a middle-aged woman huddling within a brown cape as if she feared someone would order her off the coach.

A companion, or an abigail, Meg speculated. At any rate, the creature sat apart from the couple and appeared to be travelling on her own, a situation which apparently contributed to her nervous state.

As the coachman cried, "All right behind?" and set his horses into motion, she waved through the window a last farewell to the two people she loved most dearly.

What sort of match would Angela make? Meg wondered as she settled into her seat. She was young and sometimes overeager, but she had enough sense, her sister hoped, to avoid any serious difficulty.

Much as she loved Angela, Meg was honest enough to admit the girl was not of such surpassing beauty as to rise to great heights. She would not be declared an Incomparable or a Diamond of the First Water by the gentlemen who spent their time at such exclusive clubs as White's and Watier's.

But Angela had charming blue eyes a shade darker than Meg's own, and pale blonde hair that never failed to please gentlemen. With her lively manner and sweetness of disposition, Angela would surely find a loving husband.

And I? Meg wondered.

She had no expectation of meeting anyone eligible in Derby. The country squire near her home was of middle age and comfortably wed, and she had met no young men of good breeding in that vicinity. No, she would most likely never marry or have children.

Never marry. Would that be so terrible? Meg had heard of women beaten by drunken husbands, and death in childbirth was not uncommon.

Why then did she feel this unexpected pain? Strange how she longed to feel a pair of masculine arms about her, and to hear a deep voice speaking to her tenderly. How arid the future looked to one who must travel it alone.

After a time, as the mail continued its relentless passage northward, Meg's thoughts strayed to her companions. The woman in the brown cloak was attempting to nap, twitching awake every few minutes and adjusting herself in an agitated manner. She muttered inaudible phrases as if conducting some form of debate. Poor thing, she looked as if she needed a warm hearth, a nice cup of tea, and a sympathetic shoulder, not a journey to some unknown situation. It was a relief when the woman dozed off at last.

The coach made few stops, and those brief. Finally, toward evening, Meg herself nodded off to sleep.

She napped fitfully through the night, from time to time sharing with Karen food and drink from the hamper Cook had sent along. The sun was well up on Tuesday morning when they arrived in Manchester.

Although she had been raised not too many miles away, Meg had never before visited the city of weavers and wished she owned a quizzing glass so that she might see it now. The only landmark she could define, by squinting mightily, was the fifteenth-century Gothic cathedral built of red stone.

Beside her, Karen fidgeted, her hands clenched tightly in her lap. The girl hadn't seen Peter in more than a year, and there was no telling if the message she'd sent had been received in time for him to meet her.

The coach entered the courtyard amid the shouts of welcome and the barking of dogs.

With the coachman's assistance, the passengers descended. Karen, displaying an unaccustomed authority, instructed that her mistress's trunk and her own valise be transferred to a private parlour. But despite her weariness from the uncomfortable night, Meg was in no hurry to retreat. She wanted to absorb whatever she could of the bustle of the great coaching inn and inhale the faint sea tang in the air.

She and Karen had proceeded only halfway across the yard when a great commotion erupted behind them. Turning, Meg saw the large form of the merchant who had travelled with them, arms waving in the air as he shouted something about a missing purse.

"What's happened?" she asked of no one in particular.

The brown-cloaked woman stopped beside them. "I don't know. Don't know at all. No need to make such a fuss."

"Did you see it?" Karen asked. "Was there a footpad? He's yelling that someone pinched his purse!"

"Most likely dropped it down his waistcoat," their companion muttered. "I do wish he'd stop carrying on so. Shouting gives me the megrim." She clutched a worn valise tightly in her hands.

"There! There she be!" To Meg's astonishment, the merchant pointed directly at them. In a trice, the trio found themselves surrounded by a constable, the innkeeper, and assorted spectators.

This could not be happening, Meg thought wildly. She experienced the same sensation of unreality as on that dreadful night less than a week ago when she cut Beau Brummell. But this time there was far more at stake, though she could not previously have imagined such a thing possible. The penalty for stealing was hanging, or transportation to Australia.

"What? This 'un 'ere?" demanded the constable, pointing at Karen.

"That, sir, is my abigail!" Meg protested.

"And who be you?" cried a lad who stood at the constable's elbow.

"Hush, Eddie, anyone can see she's a lady." The constable turned to the woman in brown. "Is this person with your party?"

"She did travel down with us from London, but I've only just made her acquaintance," Meg admitted. It occurred to her that she might have saved the woman a spot of trouble by claiming a relationship, but surely the creature's innocence could be quickly established.

"That must be the one." The infuriated merchant singled out the nervous woman. "Sitting right by me. I had my purse last time we stopped and now it's gone. Ten pounds in gold coin!"

An appreciative murmur rose from the crowd.

"Hand it over, then," the constable demanded, fixing the woman with a keen stare.

"I don't...I haven't..." To Meg's alarm, the woman began trembling violently. "I haven't touched his purse! We don't even know that he ever had such a thing. Why me? I knew no good would come of leaving London! My charges begged me to stay, but the doctor said I needed fresh air. Now look what they're trying to do!" Her thin frame shook with sobs.

"Oh, dear." Meg reached out and touched the woman's shoulder, trying to steady her. "I'm sure there's been some misunderstanding."

"Maybe you're in league with her, then!" the merchant snapped. "Give it here or I'll see the both of you swing."

"Watch your tongue." Karen stepped protectively forward. "My mistress is a lady and you're no gentleman, anyone can see that."

"Now, now." The constable held up his hands. "There's the matter of a missing purse to be settled."

"Arthur! Yoo-hoo, my dear!" The merchant's solidly built wife leaned out of the coach, waving something. "It was here on the floor, my sweet! Must have dropped out while you were sleeping."

"Oh, well," the fellow blustered, "no harm done then." The spectators snorted, clearly torn between amusement and disappointment.

"No harm?" Meg said. "Look at this poor woman." Indeed, the creature in the brown cape had quite dissolved into a fit of trembling, to the extent that she would have fallen had not Meg and Karen supported her.

"Apologies, miss," muttered the merchant.

"What am I to do?" A plaintive whine issued from between the woman's teeth, which were none too straight. "I cannot go on, I simply cannot. It was wrong from the start. I must return. Oh, please—" she grasped Meg's arm "—I haven't the fare back to London. I must . . . my charges . . . I simply cannot . . . God help me, what am I to do?"

Meg leveled a stare at the merchant. "This is your doing, sir."

"Well, I hardly thought . . ." He shifted uncomfortably from one foot to the other. "Oh, dash it, I'll pay the blasted fare, Martha!" This to his wife. "Come and help here. Yes, yes, we'll see she gets back all right. Why are all these people standing around? Go on, the lot of you! If you want a show, you'll have to pay admission!"

The crowd dispersed reluctantly, and the brown-cloaked woman was entrusted into Martha's care. Much relieved, Meg yielded to Karen's demands that they retire into the inn.

With more self-possession than she had ever shown before, Karen soon established Meg in a private parlour and went out to secure a post chaise to Derby and to see about her own transportation to Liverpool.

The tea and biscuits provided by the inn proved better than tolerable, but Meg nodded off to sleep before she could finish them. When Karen returned some time later, Meg awoke with a start. "Is everything set?" she asked.

"Oh, yes, miss!" cried Karen. "I've found a wagon driver from Liverpool, said Peter asked him to look out for me, but he's leaving right away. Your post chaise has to change horses, and the coachman says he wants a spot of food, and then he'll call for you. Will that be all right, miss?"

"Yes, that sounds fine." Even a woman who couldn't see properly could hardly get lost if the coachman came to fetch her personally. "Good luck, Karen." She handed the maid a small silver locket. "A wedding present."

"Thank you, miss!" Karen flung her arms around her mistress. "You've been so good to me! I'll write to you from Canada, as long as you don't mind the misspellings!"

"Indeed not." This farewell was even sadder than the ones in London, as Karen and her Peter would most likely never come back to England. A tear slipped down Meg's face and she made no attempt to stop it.

After Karen left, Meg found she couldn't go back to sleep. Indeed, she realized with a jolt, this was the first time in her gently bred life that she had ever been entirely on her own, without the protection of a servant or relative.

Though it would surely be a matter of only half an hour, or perhaps an hour at most, before the driver came for her, Meg listened carefully to every noise in the hallway. She had read stories of women menaced in isolated castles, and while she wasn't so cork-brained as to expect dark-cloaked villains in the hallway, it was true that inns sheltered all manner of people. Nervously, Meg rose and bolted the door.

If only she could see better! Then she might go downstairs—not into the taproom, of course, but in a place within public view where none could threaten her. But in her state of comparative helplessness, she was far better off here.

Her thoughts returned to the scene outside. What would have transpired had not the merchant's purse turned up? That poor woman might have been arrested; perhaps even Meg and Karen with her. There were frequent hangings in London, gleefully attended by cheering masses. Could such a thing really happen to innocent women?

Never before had she realized how sheltered her life was. Compared to the danger of arrest, the scandal which had loomed so large a scant time earlier now faded to insignificance.

In this parlour far from London, Meg could see the members of the ton for the foolish, artificial people they really were. Such fuss over Beau Brummell, whose only accomplishments were his choice of a tailor and his rapier wit! How absurd that the highest lords and ladies should shun a woman merely because she failed to acknowledge his greeting!

The first few months of this past season had been met with hope and eager expectation. At each ball she imagined she might become the latest sensation, or at least discover a man who would meet her heart's needs.

Now Meg could see that she had become disenchanted even before her ridiculously aggrandized scandal. Perhaps her departure was a blessing in disguise. But what lay ahead?

A rapping at the door roused her to herself.

"Yes?" She wondered if the pounding of her heart could be heard by the unseen visitor.

"Begging your pardon, ma'am, but the innkeeper said there was a Miss Lindsay here and I'm sent to fetch her to her carriage," said a polite male voice.

Much relieved, Meg drew the bolt and opened the door. Before her stood a coachman exquisitely clad in black-and-silver livery. It was beyond any uniform she would have expected for a post chaise driver, but no doubt this fellow took pride in appearances, and Meg could only think well of him for that.

"I've been expecting you," she said, willing to overlook his mispronouncing the name *Linley* as *Lindsay*. In her experience, a common mistake among tradesmen.

"This is your trunk then, miss?" In a trice, the driver and a young groom carried the cases downstairs, with Meg hurrying in their wake. To her surprise, the driver insisted upon paying the innkeeper for the parlour. "I've got my instructions," he said when she protested, and Meg silently thanked Karen for her thoughtfulness.

The bustle in the courtyard was as great this afternoon as it had been in the morning. Meg could perceive little beyond a great blur of motion and colour, with high-perch phaetons weaving perilously between rude wagon-carts.

"This way, miss," said the driver, taking Meg's arm to help her into the chaise.

"What a smart carriage," she said, impressed by the gleaming black-trimmed silver paint. She even thought, as he opened the door, that there might have been a coat of arms on it, but she couldn't be sure. Perhaps the crest of the inn, she told herself.

"Yes, indeed, ma'am." Despite the correctness of his reply, there was a puzzled note in the coachman's voice as he closed the door.

The interior was as elegantly appointed as the rest of the coach. Meg detected not even a sign of wear in the red velvet of the squabs. This was superior transportation indeed!

She hadn't been able to see the horses well, but the easy movement of the chaise made it evident that they were well-matched and a quick-stepping team. Again, Meg marvelled at the fine service in Manchester. London certainly had a great deal to learn!

Relieved of the fears which had plagued her at the inn, Meg gazed out with curiosity as they rumbled along. Impossible to recognize any landmarks, but that was only to be expected in her case. Still, she enjoyed the rich green colours of rural Cheshire.

The carriage halted much sooner than she'd expected. She squinted through the windows. They had pulled up in the driveway of a great Tudor house, its white-painted plaster set off by a darkened latticework of timbers.

She realized then that wherever they were, they most certainly weren't in Derby.

CHAPTER FOUR

THE MOST HONOURABLE Andrew Harwood Davis, the Marquis of Bryn, laid aside the quill pen with which he had been inscribing a letter to his man of affairs in London.

Surely, he reflected wearily as he franked the letter, it should not be necessary for him to make a trip personally on the matter of a marriage settlement. Standish should be able to send him the necessary figures and considerations by post.

The marquis rose from behind the heavy oak desk and moved to the window of his study, gazing through the many-paned glass and over the broad lawns of Brynwood. He would prefer never to visit town again, although one could not forever put aside the duty to resume one's seat in the House of Lords.

Once he was married, at least he might be spared the attentions of ambitious mothers and their insipid, giggling daughters, Bryn reflected. He could barely tolerate the thought of London society and its petty self-absorption these past two years.

He turned back to face the dark, masculine room which so perfectly reflected his own appearance. Not a bit of frippery was to be seen among the leather-covered chairs and stern bookcases.

What changes would a wife make? Andrew wondered, leaning back against the desk. None, he hoped, at least not the wife he planned to take.

Germaine Geraint was far from missish, more interested in her horses than in her draperies, he suspected from their one brief encounter at a house party. She ought to blend into his countrified existence with scarcely a ripple.

His interest in her might have struck the casual observer as perfunctory, but Lord Bryn had no jumped-up notions of romance. Marriage for a wealthy nobleman must be a means of securing heirs, with a respectable-enough mate to assure their future acceptance into society.

The marquis put no credence in amorous tomfoolery, and neither, he was pleased to note, did the lady to whom he meant to declare his intentions. Nevertheless, he must order up some new coats and trousers from Weston, who had his measure, and boots from Hoby's. The marquis glanced down at the aging pair of Hessians he wore. They suited him well enough, but his valet should have remarked on their condition long ago. If Harry were still alive...

A vise squeezed the marquis's conscience. Harry would indeed have been alive, had it not been for the vainglory two years ago of a young nodcock named Andrew Davis.

The butler knocked lightly at the door and entered. "Begging your pardon, my lord," said Franklin, "but the children have vanished."

"Vanished?" repeated Bryn.

"Bertha was watching them—the new upstairs maid, my lord—and they placed a certain small animal about her person." The butler cleared his throat, and Bryn wondered if he might be covering a chuckle.

"Small animal?" When it came to the misdeeds of his niece and nephew, Bryn frequently found himself repeating words in disbelief.

"A mouse, I believe," said the butler. "In her, er, consternation over the creature, she lost sight of them, and now they are nowhere to be found."

"Search the house," instructed his lordship.

"That has been done." Franklin betrayed a hint of exasperation. "We know their hiding places, my lord, and they are not in them."

How one seven-year-old girl and one five-year-old boy could create such a continual gallimaufry, Lord Bryn could not imagine. In the eighteen months since his sister and her husband died in a carriage accident, the children had demolished no fewer than three governesses.

"Then search the grounds," he said.

"Yes, my lord, we are doing so," replied Franklin. "However, I thought you might wish to be informed."

"How long have the children been missing?"

"Three hours, my lord."

That was a long time for two such small children. "They may have got themselves in too deep this time." The marquis pushed away from his desk. "I'll take King Arthur and join the search."

A few minutes later, he was urging the roan stallion forward. This time his young charges might be in serious difficulty, and if night fell before they were rescued, their misadventure could prove fatal.

The rolling countryside of the Cheshire Plain was deceptive. One had the impression that one could see everything for miles, but in truth clumps of trees provided more than ample hiding for a pair of tots. There were also here and there crumbling Roman fortifications. Most were located high on wooded ridges, beyond the distance a child might hike in a few hours.

But Bryn knew well from his own childhood that one could stumble upon an intriguing pile of rocks in the most unlikely places. Of these innocent-seeming ruins, more than one had tumbled in treacherously upon a curious child. He had barely escaped injury in such an accident himself.

Tom and Vanessa. They'd been entrusted to him. Had he failed them as tragically as he'd failed Harry?

Distressed, the marquis spurred his horse on toward the town of Marple. He doubted the children had got that far, but there was always the chance they had become lost on the moors.

Prior to the past year and a half, it had been Lord Bryn's impression that his niece and nephew were angelic sprites who, done up in bows and ruffles, descended from their nursery to bow and curtsey silently to their elders before retreating.

He had never been more mistaken in his life.

Perhaps the problem was the governesses one could secure, living so far from London. Well, Standish had apparently found the solution to that, and if the woman were on the mail coach as planned, she should be arriving at Brynwood that same evening.

And a welcome sight she would be, too, especially if she proved the equal of this pair of scalawags.

As the sun sank toward the west, the marquis's spirits lowered accordingly. After shouting their names until he was nearly hoarse, he rode back by the house to be sure the children hadn't been found. They had not.

Darkness would soon arrive, he thought worriedly, heading south this time. "Tom! Vanessa!" His voice mingled with the thud of King Arthur's hooves against the soft earth.

Damn. His blasted leg was beginning to hurt where the bullet had nicked the bone. The pain brought with it, as always, a double hurt, the memory of one hot humid August day on the coast of Portugal two years before.

Fresh from his triumphs in the ballrooms of London, the swaggering young Lord Bryn—as he unflatteringly considered his younger self—had set out with Wellington's troops to teach that Frenchman, Bonaparte, a lesson in English courage.

The scene blurred, as the marquis rode through the gathering twilight shouting the youngsters' names. So long ago, so far away...

The horse leaped a fence and jolted his rider's sore leg. The renewed torment brought the event back sharply.

Andrew could hear again the shouts and see the white summer uniforms of the French advancing toward the scarlet-clad British. Volleys of shots rang out; pain seared through his leg. He fell into the dirt as the columns broke and bayonets flashed around him in the sunlight.

Then someone dragged him off the battlefield. Harry. Where had he come from? Bryn had meant to order the valet to stay safely on board ship. But in his excitement at the forthcoming battle, he'd forgotten.

A shot rang out nearby, and Harry fell. Moments later, the French fled the field, momentarily defeated. But for one loyal servant from Cheshire, the respite came too late.

If I'd commanded him to stay behind, we'd both have been safe, Bryn thought for the hundredth time. *But I never gave him a thought. I was too full of my own pride to worry about Harry.*

A small cry blotted out his memories. "Uncle Andrew!" Faint, but unmistakable.

Bryn reined in King Arthur and turned east. He spotted a grove of trees, and emerging from it were two grubby urchins, their faces smeared with purple.

"Berries!" cried Vanessa, the eldest, holding up juice-stained hands.

"You should be whipped, the pair of you!" The marquis tried to hide his relief. The children needed discipline badly, and he'd never been able to bring himself to administer it, not after their tragic loss.

"But they taste so wonderful!" Tom stopped behind his sister, eyes round with delight. "Only it got late."

"We were only adventuring," said Vanessa primly. "Like the knights of old."

"Now where did you hear about that?" Charmed in spite of himself, Bryn descended to collect his errant charges.

"Miss Smithers. Or was it Miss James?" Vanessa shrugged. "One of the governesses liked to tell us stories."

"Was that the one you poured ink over, or the one you frightened off by pretending to be ghosts in the secret passage?" demanded his lordship, grasping each youngster firmly by the collar.

The children exchanged startled glances. "I didn't tell!" Tom cried.

"Well, it certainly wasn't me!" returned Vanessa.

"Despite what you may think, we adults were once children, too," said Lord Bryn, depositing Tom to the front of the saddle and Vanessa to the rear. "I want none of your nonsense with your new governess, do you understand? Or there'll be no pony at Christmas, Vanessa!"

"I promise," she said at once.

Mounting carefully between them, Lord Bryn reflected grimly that Christmas was a long time off, and children's memories were notoriously short.

They set out at a canter. Despite the long search that afternoon, King Arthur maintained a creditable pace and the trio arrived at Brynwood in time to see a young woman descending from his lordship's carriage.

"It's her!" shrilled Tom. "Look, Vanny, our new governess." There was a note of calculation in his young voice, as if he were already probing for weaknesses.

And a wonderful sight we make, the marquis thought, glancing at the children's berry-stained faces. He guided the horse into the drive and halted, taking a good look at his new employee.

Standish had described a female of three and thirty, but Bryn would have put her age at considerably less. Furthermore, his man of affairs had given him to believe the woman possessed a starchy air, but this chit looked distinctly bewildered. Moreover, he noticed as he descended and lifted down the two delighted youngsters, the new governess had a squint. Was it vanity that prevented her wearing a glass? But what use had a governess for vanity?

"Miss Lindsay!" Vanessa dashed across the drive and flung herself at the woman without the least care for what damage her dirty hands might wreak. "I'm Vanessa, and this is Tom, and that's Uncle Andrew. We're so-o-o-o glad you're here. Aren't we, Tom?" This last remark was accompanied by a conspiratorial poke.

The governess looked not the least discomfited by this assault. "I'm pleased to make your acquaintance," she said with a hint of a twinkle. "Miss Vanessa, is it? And Master Tom. My name is Miss Linley, not Lindsay."

Vanessa and Tom executed their well-rehearsed curtsey and bow respectively, only their giggles spoiling the effect.

"This be Lord Bryn," said the coachman as Andrew approached.

A startled expression flashed across the chit's face. "Lord Bryn?" she said.

Far too pretty for a governess, he thought sternly. Light brown curls peeped out of her bonnet, and her features were entirely too fine. Well, it didn't signify here in the country; there was no mistress of the house to be jealous, and no nearly grown son to go all cow-eyed over her.

Unaccountably, the marquis found himself disconcerted as the girl took in his grimy appearance. "It is not my custom to greet new arrivals in this condition," his lordship apologized, willing to extend his politeness beyond the customary level due a member of one's staff. He devoutly hoped to induce the woman to stay on at least until he took a wife. "However, the children and I were, er, having a bit of an adventure."

"That sounds delightful." The woman eyed him in a peculiar manner, as if she were trying to puzzle something out, or perhaps to make up her mind about some matter.

"I assure you, they're ordinarily well-behaved." The marquis hoped this slight untruth might be forgiven, for it would be unkind to frighten the woman. Still, she didn't look the sort who panicked easily.

Miss Linley—deuced careless of Standish to get her name wrong—glanced at the eager, dirty faces staring up at him. "I should be surprised if they were too well-behaved," she said. "It isn't in the nature of children."

"No doubt you know best in that regard," agreed the marquis, determined to be affable. "Standish assures me you have excellent references."

"I beg your pardon?"

"As a governess." What was wrong with the girl? Perhaps it was the strain of travel; he could only hope so. A nitwit wouldn't last five minutes with these little ruffians.

"Ah. A governess." She nodded, as if to herself.

"You are Myra Lindsay—excuse me, Linley—are you not?" inquired the marquis.

"Actually, my name is Margaret," replied the young woman. "And you are quite certain that you are Lord Bryn?"

No doubt she meant to be humorous. A peculiar method of going on for a woman of her station. "So my servants tell me," he responded in kind.

The marquis noted with relief the approach of the butler and housekeeper. "Mrs. Franklin, be so good as to show Miss Linley to her room. And then have Bertha—no, not Bertha—someone give these urchins a bath."

"Yes, my lord. Shall I bring tea to your study?"

"That would be splendid."

Ensconced in his study with a hearty tea of sandwiches and fresh-baked scones, Lord Bryn reflected on the peculiar demeanour of the new governess.

A bit of a quiz, indeed. He could have sworn he'd seen a squint, although she'd unscrewed her face as soon as he drew near. Standish hadn't said anything about weak eyes.

No matter. She liked the children, and they appeared to share her sentiment. Temporarily, at least. He had no illusions on that score.

How did she feel about small animals, particularly mice and frogs? Hardly the sort of question one's man of affairs was likely to have posed, but she did seem the matter-of-fact sort, not easily frightened off.

Why, he wondered, would a girl as pretty as that be content to work as a governess? Why had she agreed to come here to Cheshire? Although the salary he offered was ample, it was scarcely enough to compensate for the charms of a beau.

Well, the private lives of the staff were none of his affair, reflected the marquis, relaxing at last. The girl's manners were impeccable, and her appearance unexceptionable.

She would do. Indeed, she would have to do.

He did wish, however, that his thoughts wouldn't keep drifting to that up-tilted chin, the lively expression on her face, and the hint of merriment in her voice. Dangerous territory for a man about to get himself leg-shackled. Moreover, Lord Bryn despised those craven fellows who inflicted themselves upon helpless female servants.

Not that Miss Linley struck him as helpless. She appeared thoroughly capable of dealing with bounders and cads.

The marquis chuckled at the thought. Yes, his new governess possessed the starch that Standish had described. She would suit the position admirably.

CHAPTER FIVE

A GOVERNESS!

Untying the strings of her bonnet, Meg sank onto the bed in a fit of laughter. Lord Bryn had mistaken her for a governess!

Why hadn't she corrected his misapprehension at once? she asked herself. Pure astonishment, perhaps. And what on earth had happened to the real Myra Lindsay?

Oh, dear. That poor woman at the posting inn. Could that have been she? It would explain why a carriage had been sent. But surely she would write to explain her change of heart. Still, it might be days, even weeks before she got round to it. The woman's distress had looked severe enough for her to require a lengthy recuperation.

Part of the reason she hadn't revealed the mistake at once, Meg admitted to herself, was the children. How dear they were, although she suspected they would display a mischievous side on closer acquaintance. At home in Derby, she had played often with the servants' children, and knew how changeable they could be—friends one moment, fierce enemies the next, and whimpering babies an instant later. It took all one's patience to deal with them, but the annoyance was quickly forgotten when they threw their arms around one and held tight.

A tap at the door announced the tea tray, and Meg greeted the maid with suitably restrained politeness. The girl stayed longer than necessary, fussing with the tray; unquestionably so as to have a few details of the new arrival to carry back to eager ears in the kitchen.

Well, now what am I going to do? she asked herself. Lord Bryn will have to let me stay the night, and then I shall be packed off to Derby.

The prospect of joining the Barkers struck her as less and less appealing after the adventures of the past few days. How tedious it would be, listening to them prose on about sin and corruption, sitting by the fireside evening after evening with a bit of embroidery in her lap and a yawn dutifully suppressed.

She did love Derby, with its beautiful churches, parks, and fine new Georgian houses. But in recent years, as her vision weakened, Meg had been unable any longer to take so much pleasure as formerly in her walks, nor did the state of her purse allow for many purchases of the city's exquisite silks.

Indeed, even were there social occasions to which she might be invited, the Barkers would never agree to chaperon her. There would be no calling cards left, and no gentleman asking to take her driving, as there had been from time to time in London.

Briefly, as she changed from her dusty travel clothes into a dark bombazine gown suitable for dinner in the country, Meg allowed herself to wonder what it would be like to be courted by Lord Bryn.

Now, why should the thought of him quicken her breath? He was said to be all but promised to Germaine Geraint, Helen Cockerell's cousin. Certainly the man had given no sign of attraction to a mere governess.

Yet there was something about the way he'd looked at her. In all honesty, Meg was forced to admit she had never seen a man quite so handsome—dark, yet not intimidating, courteous yet not obsequious. There was an honesty to his face which she liked at once, and a masculine set to his shoulders which made her wonder instinctively how it would feel to be held in those strong arms.

Stuff and nonsense. She'd never been given to excessive daydreaming. And of all men, the reclusive Lord Bryn was far beyond her reach. She would be best to guard her thoughts, and her heart.

Still fighting the memory of those grave, gentle eyes, Meg pinned up her locks with more skill than most women of her station could have managed, for the Linleys' lack of funds made a hairdresser a rare luxury. It struck her that, with her practical turn, she might serve well as a governess, if such a thing did not prove an embarrassment to her mother.

Such musings were neither here nor there. She was not a governess, nor was she the woman who had been expected today. As soon as possible, she must tell the marquis the truth.

Ruefully Meg reflected on how to accomplish that. What could she say? Excuse me, sir, I am a lady with weak eyesight who entered your carriage by mistake. Indeed, I am the fool who set all London a-twitter, by my bumblings. Pray excuse me and send me home.

But the real governess had turned back. Who would care for the children? Meg knew enough of the usual manner of treating staff to recognize that his lordship's politeness toward her betrayed a growing desperation with his young charges.

Those berry-stained faces! She chuckled softly, remembering them. They might need a firm hand, but at heart they were good youngsters. If only she could have such children someday.

If I am not to marry, I shall never have children at all.

The thought was too painful to be borne. Swiftly Meg rose and slipped on the sensible shoes from her trunk. The clothes she'd brought were plain enough for a governess, that much was true.

Another knock at the door admitted the housekeeper, Mrs. Franklin. "Is everything to your satisfaction, Miss Linley?" she inquired.

"Yes, thank you," she said.

"It's an excellent room," the woman continued. "Have you noticed the view from the windows? In the daylight one can see halfway across Cheshire."

"Indeed?" Courtesy obliged Meg to join Mrs. Franklin by the curtains, but the deepening twilight revealed only indistinct shapes. "I, er, fear I misplaced my lorgnette on the journey. My eyes are a bit weak."

"Oh, my, what a shame, and you so young!" declared the housekeeper. "Now let me think. The late Lady Bryn, Lord Andrew's mother, had a glass. Perhaps I could find it, if you like. I doubt his lordship would object."

"Could you?" This turn of events was an unexpected blessing. "I'd be most grateful."

"Certainly." Mrs. Franklin smiled warmly, and Meg began to wish she really were the governess and could stay in this hospitable place for a time. "Now, would you care to see the nursery and the schoolroom before dinner?"

"Yes, indeed." Much as she hated to deceive the kindly woman, Meg considered it improper to confide in her before revealing the truth to the marquis.

"His lordship is expecting you for dinner," added Mrs. Franklin as the two women climbed to the second floor together.

Meg nodded. Some households, particularly in the country, included the governess as one of the family for informal occasions, although she would never have been invited to dine with guests.

From the musty smell of the schoolroom, it had not been used for some time. "When did the last governess leave?" she asked.

"Two months ago," replied the housekeeper.

"May I ask why?"

"Peculiar woman." Mrs. Franklin led the way back into the hall. "Declared she heard ghosts walking at night. I cannot imagine what made her think so. Brynwood has never been haunted."

"Except perhaps by children," murmured Meg.

They proceeded into the nursery, where the youngsters were dining at a small table. As soon as they entered, Tom jumped to his feet and ran toward Meg. "Miss Linley! May I show you my collection of bugs? I've pressed them so neatly—"

"Enough o' that, Master Tom." A beefy serving woman caught the youngster deftly by the collar and hauled him back into place.

"Thank you, Jenny," said Mrs. Franklin.

The children hurriedly finished eating and came to sit beside Meg on a padded bench. "We'll leave you for a few minutes, then," said the housekeeper, and Jenny followed her out.

"Would you like to see my bugs?" asked Tommy.

"Oh, yes. I adore bugs." Meg forced herself not to flinch as he produced a wooden box filled with dried flattened specimens. "You must tell me all their names."

"I dunno their names," he said. "Do you?"

"That is a six-legged bug-opterus," Meg improvised, pointing, but not able to bring herself to actually touch the crusty thing. "And that is a hard-shelled thing-a-ma-bob."

Tommy regarded her sceptically. "You don't act much like a governess."

"What makes you so certain I am one?" Meg replied with equal gravity.

"Well, of course you are!" said Vanessa. "What else would you be?"

"Perhaps a lady of fashion?" Meg suggested.

"Then what would you be doing here?" the girl demanded.

"Well—" Meg pretended to rack her brains "—perhaps I was on a journey when your coachman mistook me for the real governess, and I mistook him for a hired post chaise driver."

"What fun!" cried Tom, stuffing the box of bugs back into the toy chest.

"Oh, don't be a goose," snapped his sister. "Everyone knows ladies don't travel alone. And no one would be such a nodcock as to mistake uncle's carriage for a post chaise!"

Meg smiled ruefully. "I'm sure you're right."

"Now we must be good hosts and show you around the nursery," announced Vanessa, standing up.

"Vanny, don't," pleaded Tom, his eyes widening. "I like her."

"Well, of course you do." Vanny had learned young to imitate her elders' hypocrisy, Meg noted; the young girl parroted polite phrases even while clearly intending mischief.

"I should be delighted to see more of your playroom," said Meg. If the children made convincing enough ghosts to frighten off the last governess, she was mightily curious to see what else they would try.

She heard a whispered conference. In compensation for her eyesight, it seemed, Meg had developed keen hearing and made out the words, "Where is it?" and "...under the chest, where it always goes."

"This way, Miss Linley." Vanessa straightened up and led the way about the large nursery, pointing out its shelves of books, the rocking horse, and a chipped music box. With aplomb, Meg shook hands with a stuffed bear and conducted a mock conversation with a china doll, pretending not to notice that its voice issued from Vanessa's mouth.

"I like her!" Tom repeated, more forcefully than before.

"Get it!" hissed his sister.

After a moment's hesitation, the boy scrambled away while Vanessa provided a diversion in the form of a curtsey. "This is how my mother taught me, Miss Linley. Do you think I'm ready to be presented at court?"

"I shouldn't be in any hurry for that if I were you," Meg said.

"Why not?"

"It's a horribly stiff affair, everyone in black dresses afraid they'll make some slip," she said. "Queen Charlotte is most imposing, and if you give offence, you are banished from London at once. Not officially, of course, but it comes to the same thing."

"You sound as if you've been there." The childish face gazed up at her with new interest.

"There, didn't I tell you I wasn't really a governess?" As she spoke, Meg felt something small and furry drop onto her foot and arch itself against her leg. "Well, what have we here?"

She knelt and scooped up the white mouse, which regarded her with beady black eyes. "What's his name?"

"Terror," admitted Vanessa, not the least abashed. Tom could only stare up at the fearless governess in awe.

"Do you know," continued Meg, who had owned a pet mouse once herself, "that he might suffer serious harm being dropped on a person's foot that way? Suppose someone kicked him off by mistake?"

"It's been done," Tom said.

"Was he injured?"

"He limped for two days, just like Uncle Andrew," the little boy said.

Meg stifled a whoop of laughter. A cat may look at a king, and a small boy make joke about the afflictions of his distinguished relative. "There. You take my meaning. If you cannot treat an animal well, you should release him to the out-of-doors.''

Carefully she lowered the rodent into Tom's outstretched hands, and watched as he tucked the animal into a wooden box punched with holes for air. ''I promise never to do it again, Miss Linley.''

Meg turned to see a triumphant look in Vanessa's eyes. ''You must be a governess!'' the little girl declared. ''A lady would have shrieked down the roof. You know all about children, don't you?''

''Not everything,'' said Meg modestly, ''but I've met a few in my time. And I was one myself once.''

''That's what Uncle Andrew always says!'' declared Tom. ''Though I don't think he was ever really a child. Not like us.''

The housekeeper returned, looking pleased to see how well the three were getting on. The maid Jenny followed her in to take charge of the youngsters' bedtime preparations, while a thoughtful Meg departed with Mrs. Franklin.

How could she leave these two children, when she'd barely got to know them? Clearly they needed guidance and a feminine touch, someone who knew when to join in their games and when to take a firm stand. Someone to help them over the difficult path to adulthood that lay ahead.

Yet it was unthinkable to masquerade as a governess! What a terrible scandal there would be if anyone should find out. She dared not even picture Lord Bryn's fury.

But Meg might never have a husband and children of her own. True, she hoped to have nieces and nephews, but they would never be entrusted directly into her care. And she could not help reflecting how much more pleasant it would be to remain at Brynwood for the rest of the season. Letters could be dispatched to the Barkers and to London, saying she had encountered an old school friend en route. Lady Mary might think it peculiar, but no doubt she would accept the situation, for at the home of a friend Meg would at least have the opportunity to meet eligible gentlemen.

Good heavens, Meg told herself, could she really be contemplating staying on? She must have taken leave of her senses! But she was already in disgrace. Didn't she deserve a little holiday from being proper for once?

Her thoughts still in turmoil, she went down to dinner.

His lordship awaited her at the foot of the stairs, offering his arm in gentlemanly fashion and leading her into the long dining room. "So formal, in the country?" she inquired, glad that at least he seated her beside him rather than at the far end of the massive oak table.

"I am accustomed to taking dinner in my study, but in honour of your arrival, I thought it would be pleasant to hold a sort of celebration." The marquis surveyed a chilled bottle of Italian wine proffered by Franklin. "Would you care for a glass?"

"Yes, thank you," said Meg, although she hardly ever drank anything stronger than ratafia.

She was starting on the soup of creamed cucumbers and wondering how to broach the subject of her identity when Lord Bryn himself took up the matter.

"When I went upstairs just now to say good-night to the urchins, I was told the most amazing tales." His brown eyes caught Meg's blue ones over the wineglasses.

"Indeed?" Her breath came rapidly. The nearness of the man was daunting. Seated so close to him, she could not help but be aware of the strong planes of his cheekbones, nor avoid noticing the way his gaze kept returning to her face.

"First of all, Thomas informs me that you sprang to the mouse's defence and chastised the children firmly for risking its life and limbs. Not the sort of conduct one normally encounters in a governess." He awaited her reply with evident interest.

"Children must learn to be kind to creatures who are weaker than they," she replied. "Besides, I once had a pet mouse myself."

"And then," said his lordship, "Vanessa told me some things I found even more unusual."

"Yes?" Now she was for it, Meg feared.

"She said that you are not a governess at all, but a lady of fashion, who has been presented at court. Wherever can she have got such ideas?" It might have been amusement lurking at the corners of his mouth, or merely a dry irony, but in either case how pleasant it would be to tease him, to joke and flirt, Meg thought, to her own surprise. She had never particularly enjoyed such pursuits in London, but then she had never met a man as magnetic as Lord Bryn.

In any event she must strive to be honest. But by the time she gathered her wits to speak, the servants arrived with venison in caper sauce, fillets of turbot, broiled mushrooms and ham fritters. She drew in a deep breath until the two of them were left alone.

"Vanessa got those ideas from me," she said, and awaited his reply with a tight squeezing sensation across her chest.

"From you?" The marquis poured himself a second glass of wine, although Meg had scarcely begun her first. "How intriguing. It might work, you know."

"Might work?" she repeated.

"The child is incorrigible," he said. "She has no respect for man or beast. Except for grand ladies, since she expects to be one."

"I would hardly call myself grand." Meg kept her speech short so that she might better enjoy the meal. To her surprise, she was ravenously hungry, and the food was excellent.

"Nevertheless, your description of Queen Charlotte appears to have made an impression," he said. "You might

turn that wild creature into a young lady yet, Miss Linley."
He saluted her with his glass before emptying it.

Meg nearly choked on a bite of the veal. He was taking all
this as a game! "Suppose it were true, my lord?"

"Beg pardon?"

"Suppose I were in fact a lady on my way from London
to Derby, and on account of my weak eyesight I mistook
your carriage for my post chaise?" There, she'd said it.

"Then what has become of the real Miss Linley? Or
Lindsay?" A glint in those dark eyes told her he was enjoying the sport.

"She, er, was falsely accused of a theft, and even though
she was proved innocent, she quite lost all her courage and
insisted upon turning back." The tale sounded impossibly
weak in Meg's own ears. "She really was a fluttery creature, not at all suited to the upbringing of such sturdy children as your wards, you see."

"Indeed." The marquis nodded in mock gravity. "Now
let me see. Ah, you haven't yet explained why a young lady
of good breeding such as yourself would be travelling un-
accompanied."

"I had brought my maid from London to Manchester,
but she left, with my blessing, to join her true love, who is
about to depart from Liverpool for Canada." Oh, dear,
thought Meg, I wouldn't even believe that one, were it told
me by the prime minister!

"Not quite up to your invention about the governess's
being accused of thievery, but excellent work for a moment's notice," said the marquis. "I must tell you, Miss
Linley, that I am delighted to find myself employing a *ra-
conteuse*."

"Suppose I'm telling the truth?" She couldn't quite bring
herself to tell him so straight out. How could she bear to
ruin the most pleasant evening she'd enjoyed in months?

"If this preposterous invention were fact," mused the marquis, "I should nevertheless beseech you to grace us with your company for at least a few months' time, for the children are desperately in need of a governess. And I—" His voice broke off, as if before some strong emotion. In that moment, for all the weakness of her eyes, Meg thought she'd glimpsed a dark sliver of despair and loneliness slipping out through his tightly controlled features.

What had the war done to this man? Was she a fool to think that he needed her, and that duty required her to stay? No, more than duty. The caged needs of her own heart answered him silently. *If there is never to be a husband, or children of my own, at least there can be this short respite. I want to be near him for a time, until I am strong enough to go my way alone.*

"I will stay a while," said Meg. Oh, Lord, what had she done? Dessert was brought in, but she scarcely tasted the Chantilly crème, and excused herself as soon as the meal was finished.

Impossible, she told herself as she hurried up the stairs. She must write the marquis a note. Giving him her parents' names would suffice to clear up the matter. Or she might even confess her friendship with Helen Cockerell, the cousin of his intended.

Yet even as she commanded herself not to remain under this roof for a second night, Meg knew that she would. He had touched a place in her buried so long that she had ceased to believe in its existence.

She turned the knob and stepped into her bedchamber, halting as she caught sight of something sparkling on the dressing table. She crossed the room, picked up the quizzing glass, which was rimmed with silver, and held it to her eye.

Around her, the room came sharply into focus. How bright the golden bed cover appeared, and how the polished lamp gleamed in its own light. How could she have failed to notice the intricate leaf pattern on the wallpaper, which now leaped out at her?

It was the most splendid lorgnette Meg had ever used. She must have it. But as the property of the late Lady Bryn, it could not possibly be taken away from the premises. Perhaps it was a sign, she told herself shakily as she began to undress.

That very evening, Meg wrote notes to her cousins and her mother and Helen, describing her delight at unexpectedly renewing old acquaintance with a dear friend and telling how she had accepted the invitation to visit for a few weeks.

CHAPTER SIX

ANGELA PASSED the evening following her sister's departure in a state of unaccustomed agitation, although she hid these emotions from her mother by keeping her head lowered over a piece of embroidery.

How terribly she missed Meg! And how she resented the shallow society which had, in effect, banished her. Those silly ladies and gentlemen would forget the incident in a week, so long as Meg was absent. Why should they levy so strong a penalty for a mere misunderstanding? Angela loathed them all. How, then, could she still yearn so to be a part of that society, to dance with handsome gentlemen and go riding in Hyde Park? Her own longings shamed her.

Lady Mary read aloud as they sat in their private parlour, a task which Meg had always fulfilled before. Angela scarcely heard the words, but she noted the dryness of her mother's voice that signalled her advancing years.

I shall do it for Mother! Angela told herself, pleased at this compromise. I shan't go about to gratify my own selfish wishes, but for all our sakes' I must find myself a husband.

Would it be all right, under the circumstances, to marry someone she did not love? Perhaps she should make a noble sacrifice...but it would hurt Meg and Lady Mary to see me unhappy, she reminded herself. With a sigh of relief, the good-hearted girl concluded that duty required her to do exactly what she most wanted, which was to go out and enjoy herself, and to find a man she could cherish.

The next morning, Angela bounded out of bed with un-accustomed enthusiasm. Vauxhall, tonight, was to be her initiation—albeit an informal one—into the exalted realm of the ton.

Upon opening the wardrobe to select appropriate apparel for the morning, Angela noticed the dresses her sister had left behind. They reminded her that she must speak with her mother about ordering new gowns for her come-out.

There would be a ball in her honour! Angela whirled around the bedroom in delight. So many wonderful things to look forward to! People arriving in carriages, dressed in their finest, and instead of peeking down from the stairwell as she had done in her childhood, Angela would be standing with Lady Mary to greet them.

She would have to wear white, of course—but that was so insipid! Perhaps ivory; the colour better flattered her fair complexion. And for her hair? A wreath of tiny roses, she decided.

Angela descended for breakfast in a splendid mood, until she remembered that Meg was not there to share her happiness. "Do you suppose it was terribly uncomfortable, spending the night on the coach?" she asked Lady Mary, helping herself to coddled eggs and ham from the sideboard.

"I cannot think it was the most pleasant night she ever spent," said her mother over a cup of coffee. In the morning light, her face looked more creased with worry than Angela had ever seen it. "But there was no helping it, and they should be arriving in Manchester shortly."

They both lapsed into silence, each with her private thoughts. How to bring up the subject on her mind without appearing insensitive, Angela wondered. "What shall I wear to Vauxhall tonight?" she inquired at last.

"The pink muslin," replied Lady Mary without thinking, as it was Angela's only presentable gown.

"Shall we call on the dressmaker today?" her daughter continued.

"Beg pardon?" said Lady Mary.

"The dressmaker," pressed Angela. "I must have gowns if I'm to come out. Do you think we'll receive vouchers for Almack's?"

"One can only hope." Lady Mary brushed a wisp of hair back from her forehead.

Angela couldn't understand why her mother failed to respond with more enthusiasm. "They cannot send the vouchers until I'm formally introduced to society, can they, Mother?"

"No, indeed." Lady Mary was listening with only half her mind.

Her daughter toyed with the food and poured out a cup of coffee for herself. "Is something amiss, Mother?"

"What?" A startled look. "No, no. I was only thinking about . . . things."

"We must make plans, for the season is almost half over," Angela pointed out. "How many new dresses shall we order? I can make do with some of Meg's clothes for riding and day wear, I think, but don't you agree I shall need new ball gowns? And we must make arrangements for the band, and the food, and of course the flowers."

Finally her mother paid full attention. "Oh, dear," she said.

That did not bode well. "Have I said something wrong?" Angela asked worriedly. "I'm only concerned that the season will be over before we begin."

"Quite right." Lady Mary pushed aside her cup and was about to speak when the maid returned to clear away the dishes. "Come upstairs, Angela. We have matters to discuss."

Matters to discuss? the girl wondered as they ascended. Always before it had been Meg who shared their mother's confidences, and she felt vaguely uneasy even as she enjoyed being treated as an adult. If only the words didn't sound so... foreboding.

Lady Mary led the way into Angela's bedroom, closed the door firmly behind them, and went to open the wardrobe. She began examining Meg's dresses. "We can have this made over." She lifted out a gown of silver gauze embroidered with tiny rosebuds. "The waistline can be raised to suit the new styles."

Angela watched in distress. "But can't I have my own ball gowns?" she asked. "Someone might recognize this one and say the Linleys are woefully pinchpenny!"

Her mother turned to face her. "Sit down, Angela," she said with a meaning look.

The girl sat in a gilt chair by the dressing table. "Have I been rude, Mother?"

"No, my dear." With a deep sigh, the older woman sat on the bed with the silver dress arrayed over her arm, forgotten. "It is time we discussed the matter of finances."

"Finances?" Angela knew nothing of bank accounts, rents, and investments, so surely her mother did not mean that.

"When your father died, I was left with a modest competence," said Lady Mary. "Enough to keep us in comfort, if we lived quietly in the country. But that would have meant no chance for either of you to marry well, and so we came to London."

It had never occurred to Angela that they could not afford their current way of life, and she stared at the parent in dismay.

"The expenses of a London season are considerable," her mother went on in the same calm voice. "Meg's come-out ball and her gowns were expensive. I'm afraid, my dear, that we cannot afford the same for you."

"We can't?" Angela's voice emerged in a squeak.

"Fortunately Meg took great care of her dresses, and they can be altered," Lady Mary went on. "Her...disgrace gives us good reason to avoid the ostentation of a ball. We shall seek some more modest means of bringing you out."

"Then I shan't be invited to Almack's?"

"Although unfortunately both your grandfathers' titles have devolved upon distant cousins, we are still well enough connected, and I have some old school friends who would speak in our behalf," her mother said. "We may yet obtain vouchers."

Angela stared glumly down at her hands. Much as she despised her own frivolity, she had looked forward to selecting fabrics for her gowns and decorations for her ball. How was a gentleman to notice her, if she were seen only at an occasional card party?

"My dear, I am terribly sorry to disappoint you," said Lady Mary. "Even Meg wasn't fully aware of how straitened our circumstances have become."

Meg. She'd gone off to Derby without protest, more than willing to give Angela her chance. The younger girl lifted her chin and met her mother's eyes squarely. "Forgive me for my selfishness." She managed to keep her voice steady. "I shall do my best to acquire a suitable husband, Mother, and I shall be honoured to wear my sister's gowns."

Seeing that Lady Mary still looked distressed, Angela distracted her by reaching for the silver gown. "You're quite right that we should raise the waistline, and supposing we add a bit of pink ribbon at the neckline and hem? No one will recognize it, not even Helen."

The stratagem proved effective, and soon mother and daughter were fully absorbed in devising ways to turn Meg's old dresses into new ones.

GAILY DECORATED LANTERNS filled the night with dabs of colour, musicians played themselves into a seeming frenzy in the golden cockle-shell at the centre of the gardens, and the wine flowed merrily in the reserved box at the Rotunda.

Assured that his sister, Helen, was enjoying herself in the company of their Aunt Emily and two young cousins, Mr. Edward Cockerell leaned back in his chair and gazed at the motley crowds circulating through Vauxhall.

A pity that anyone could enter—the cost was a mere pittance—he reflected, noting a pair of ruffians who swaggered across the grass, freely eyeing the ladies. Ranelagh had been far more exclusive and elegant, which was perhaps why it had closed for lack of funds six years before, when Edward was three and twenty.

"Look!" Helen poked her brother in the ribs, startling him so that he nearly overturned his chair. "There's Lady Darnet!"

Edward felt himself blush a deep unaccustomed scarlet, aware that his sister's voice had been heard by everyone at their table.

"Who's Lady Darnet?" squealed their twelve-year-old cousin Rachel, who, with her brother and mother, was their house guest for the summer.

"That lady over there." With her ivory fan, Helen pointed to a tall young woman walking on the arm of an older man.

Cynthia Darnet, married at eighteen to a count and widowed childless a year ago at seven and twenty, had been esteemed an Incomparable at her come-out. And as Edward well knew, the intervening years had in no way dimmed her cool beauty, accentuated by her dark upswept hair and glacially serene grey eyes.

"Who's that man with her?" piped up Cousin Teddy, with the gusto of an unrestrained ten-year-old.

"One of her suitors, I expect." Helen cast a sideways glance at her brother, and Edward cleared his face of all expression.

It was no secret that he sometimes called upon Lady Darnet since her emergence from mourning. A man had a duty to wed, and with the great age of thirty looming before him, Edward intended to fulfill his familial obligations. Lady Darnet was by far the most likely prospect among his acquaintance.

"Looks cold as a mackerel to me," declared Rachel. "Do you notice how she barely nods to the people she knows?"

"How do you know whether she knows them?" inquired Teddy.

Helen laughed and answered for Rachel, "If she didn't, she wouldn't acknowledge them at all!"

"Nor should she," Edward felt obliged to rebuke. Sometimes his sister's manner was entirely too lighthearted. "Lady Darnet knows how to conduct herself properly."

"Starched up." The words appeared to have come from Aunt Emily, although the heavy-set woman hardly ever spoke.

"Beg pardon?" said Edward, but his aunt gave no sign of noticing.

"I didn't mean to criticize her," Helen put in quickly. "I know you're fond of her, Edward, and she's certainly a beauty. If only she would unbend a little! I'm sure she's perfectly charming when one comes to know her."

Edward lapsed into silence, uncertain how to respond, for he had never developed a close enough friendship with Lady Darnet to discover whether she was charming or not.

Should he rise now and approach the widow? Perhaps her escort was merely an old friend or relative. Could she seriously allow herself to be courted by someone so old? But then, her late husband the earl had been elderly, Edward recalled.

Suddenly he realized that he'd been spotted. The countess and her companion were headed toward the Cockerell
box. An honour indeed!

"Oh, there they are! Over here!" cried Helen, but she
wasn't waving at Lady Darnet.

Edward followed her gaze and saw with a shock the figures of Lady Mary Linley and her younger daughter approaching them, with a groom following at a respectful
distance. At the same moment, Lady Darnet observed the
pair headed in the same direction and halted. After a moment's hesitation, she and her escort moved off.

"You haven't invited them to join us!" cried Edward.
"Helen, what can you be thinking?"

"Oh, hush, Edward." It was definitely Aunt Emily who
spoke this time.

"Why?" One could almost see Rachel's ears prick up.
"What's wrong with them? Why is Lady Icicle turning
away?"

The Linleys were upon them, and with a flurry the group
shifted about. Additional chairs were sent for to accom-
modate the new arrivals. Safely ensconced among their
friends, Lady Mary signalled the groom that he might wan-
der off and amuse himself for the next few hours.

Even Rachel knew enough not to ask rude questions, and
for a time the talk was of such impersonal matters as sing-
ers at the Opera and the latest fashions.

The Linley chit kept her eyes lowered and said little. Milk-
and-water miss indeed, not yet properly come out, Edward
recalled. Reserve could be a good quality in a woman, as
Lady Darnet demonstrated, but insipidness was not to be
tolerated.

He himself maintained a chill politeness with the Linleys. Lady Mary merited one's respect by reason of her
breeding and connections; had she been alone, no doubt the
countess and her companion would have joined the party.

But to bring along this odious young girl, on the heels of her sister's disgrace! Whatever had Helen been thinking of, to invite them over?

The more he looked at the girl, the more Edward took her in dislike. How dared she be so pretty, with golden-blonde curls, deep blue eyes, and a hint of a smile playing perpetually around her full lips? She ought to be downcast and mousy!

Nor could he help noticing how others of their acquaintance avoided the group, staring in amazement as Helen and Lady Mary carried on a lively conversation.

What were they speaking of now? Something about Meg going off to the country. And a dashed good thing, too! If only her sister had gone along!

"Edward!" Helen rapped her brother's arm. "Woolgathering? If you've nothing to contribute to the conversation, then I suggest you dance with Angela."

Edward was too stunned to reply, and before he knew what he was about, he found himself standing up with the young lady as the band launched into a gavotte. The proposal being too awkward to decline, he offered his arm to the simpering thing and led her onto the grass, where sets were forming. Once again, he caught the disapproving gaze of Lady Darnet upon them.

Not that he had developed a tendre for the widow, but Edward prided himself on serving as a model of respectability. He had hoped to secure a wife who would follow his example, and Lady Darnet was perfect for the role. If he'd lost his chance with her, it was because of this encroaching young mushroom!

Edward was hard put not to glare as they moved through the figure of the dance. Why did Angela have to be so graceful, and dimple so prettily when she curtseyed? It must give Lady Darnet entirely the wrong idea.

The end of the dance brought with it considerable relief, until Angela said, "If you would be so kind, Mr. Cockerell, you could do me a great favour."

"Yes?" he asked irritably.

"I've heard so much about the lovely walks one can take about the grounds, but they say it's dangerous without a gentleman escort," said Angela. "Could you show me one of the paths?"

Edward glared at her. "Do you realize how improper that request is, young woman?"

The blue eyes widened with alarm. "No. Why?"

Edward steered her to one side, where they were not so directly in public view. "That is not a place where a gentleman takes a lady, unless they are betrothed," he said. "Improper things may occur."

"Oh." Angela bit her lip, gazing up at him with that annoyingly innocent demeanour. "I do beg your pardon, Mr. Cockerell."

"Furthermore, if you had the least regard for common decency—" He stopped himself abruptly, but the harm was done.

"Pray finish your sentence." A dangerous note lurked beneath the chit's calm voice.

"I should not have spoken." He offered his arm to return her to the box, but she stood as if planted. "Miss Angela, I hope you are not about to make an unpleasant scene?"

"I wasn't the one who spoke of regard for common decency," she snapped. "Pray explain yourself, sir."

From across the grass, Lady Darnet was watching this conversation with a deepening frown. "I spoke out of turn," Edward said, wishing only to end the confrontation. "Now let us go back."

"Not yet." Angela took a deep breath. "I know people are avoiding us, and I understand that this is embarrassing to you, Mr. Cockerell."

"Indeed." He could not abandon the girl, and so must hear her out.

"But I had expected Helen's brother to be less...less...judgemental, particularly when he is unacquainted with the facts," she finished in a rush.

"Oh?" This had gone far enough, Edward decided. "I believe I know enough of what happened to form my own conclusion, for I myself was present at Almack's Wednesday last. Your sister, who has established a reputation for haughtiness unbefitting her station, intentionally cut a close friend of the Prince Regent, in full view of the cream of society."

Angela was on the point of responding when she appeared to recall something and bit her lip. "There are matters I cannot speak of, but you are being most unfair."

"No, I am not." Matters she could not speak of, indeed! Did she wish him to believe Brummell had insulted her sister? Not likely! "But your private affairs are your business. As concerns Helen, however, I will thank you to avoid her presence in public lest she, too, finds herself ostracized."

"Oh, indeed!" Anger fired through those blue eyes, turning them a deep turquoise. "Your sister thinks differently!"

"My sister is too young to know much of the ton," replied Edward, pleased at having regained the offensive. "She is not so unassailable as to be above reproach, should she be linked with you."

"And you think so highly of these friends of yours, who condemn and reject others for some imagined infraction of their rules?" she demanded. "And you wish your sister similarly to abandon her dearest bosom bows to suit the false opinions of others?"

"You are an ignorant child," he returned haughtily. "Miss Angela, you are not even out yet, and I think it best that you remain that way until next season."

"No, I shall not!" She stamped one small foot in frustration. "Such pettiness! Such meanness of spirit! I had always thought elegant gentlemen like yourself to be noble and just, and you are a grave disappointment to me, Mr. Cockerell!"

The thrust took him aback. How dare this little nobody chastise him this way? Yet at the same time, Edward felt a peculiar twinge of dismay, that he should have been thought to be one of high standards and found wanting.

"Very well, I shall demonstrate my fairness," he said, holding himself rigidly erect. "Explain to me how I have misunderstood your sister's conduct, which I myself witnessed."

Angela swallowed and glanced over at her mother, but Lady Mary was facing the other direction.

"Come, come," Edward pressed. "The next dance will begin soon! We cannot stand here all night."

The girl faced him again, looking grimly determined. "You must promise me that nothing of what I say will be repeated to anyone save your sister, who already knows of it."

"Very well." Edward prickled with curiosity, a trait he had done his best to suppress, for he despised gossip. But this was no rumour; he was speaking with the subject's own sister. "I will repeat nothing."

Angela cleared her throat, a childlike gesture which he found oddly appealing. "Meg has . . . weak eyes."

Edward, who had been expecting some thunderous revelation, regarded her in perplexity. "Beg pardon?"

"She cannot see well," the girl explained. "She did not see Mr. Brummell."

"He was directly in front of her!"

"Nevertheless, she did not see him, and Mother refuses to allow her a lorgnette." Angela squared her shoulders. "If she had worn a quizzing glass to Almack's, what would people have said?"

"That she was young to have lost her vision and would make a poor wife," Edward admitted. "Or at least, some of them might have said so."

"There you are!" Angela said. "It's disgraceful, the way women are paraded about in the marriage mart! Like horses at Tattersall's, as if a happy marriage were based on the length of one's shank and the colour of one's coat!"

"You must not speak that way," he reproved in a low voice. "It is most unseemly."

"I beg your pardon if I've given offence." Angela didn't look in the least contrite. "But it's true. What choice had my sister? She must go in public without a lorgnette, and then she is censured when she fails to acknowledge someone!"

There was some justice to her viewpoint, Edward had to admit. "I suppose she cannot be held at fault, if the slight were inadvertent."

"Yet if she were to confess its cause, she would be no less harmed," said Angela. "Indeed, a scandal may be forgotten, but weak eyesight endures forever!"

This touch of pomposity issuing from those earnest lips startled a chuckle from Edward. He could see why she amused his sister.

"You have made your point, Miss Angela," he conceded. "I apologize for my remark, although I had no way of knowing of your sister's weakness. I don't agree that she would be so scorned as you think for wearing a lorgnette, although no doubt some would find her wanting. In any event, I shan't begrudge you Helen's companionship."

"Thank you." She laid her hand on his arm rather stiffly, and together they walked back to the box.

If Edward thought he had finished with the business of the Linleys, however, he was very much mistaken. Not more than a half hour later, Helen clapped her hands together and said, "I have it! Edward, we shall introduce Angela to society ourselves!"

"You've gone mad!" he declared before he could stop himself.

"Edward!" cried his sister in horror.

For the second time that evening, he blushed deeply. "Lady Mary, my apologies."

"Indeed!" Helen glared at her brother and then pressed her advantage. "We shall give a garden party at our house in Kensington next week for that purpose. Everyone knows how lovely our gardens are at this time of year, and furthermore, they will attend out of curiosity if for no other reason."

"You are too kind." Lady Mary looked as if she would prefer to decline, but dared not.

"Helen, you're wonderful!" Angela flung her arms around the older girl.

Under ordinary circumstances Edward would have refused to consider it. This project was most ill-advised and could harm both his and his sister's prospects for an advantageous match. Indeed, he suspected his suit with Lady Darnet was near lost already.

Yet after his rude remark in front of Lady Mary, he could not object again, particularly now that he understood the elder daughter had been blameless. "Very well," he said at last, with what grace he could summon.

It was with relief that Edward rose to bid the Linleys good-night, and watched them walk away with their protective groom. His gaze lingered for a moment on the figure of Miss Angela. What a surprise she had turned out to be, standing up to him that way! Her vigorous defence of a beloved sister spoke well for her, and brought out his most chivalrous instincts.

This business of a garden party was going entirely too far, but they had promised, and he could not back out.

Well, thought Edward as he resumed his seat, after next week he would avoid the unpredictable Miss Angela. If fortune smiled, perhaps she might make a match quickly with some younger son of a lord, and retire from the social scene.

Why that thought did not entirely please him, he could not have said.

CHAPTER SEVEN

MEG AWOKE EARLY on Wednesday, blinking her eyes in confusion as she studied her comfortable surroundings. Where was she? This certainly wasn't the bedroom she shared with Angela in London, nor was it the attic room of their cottage in Derby.

Lord Bryn! She sat bolt upright. Good heavens, it hadn't been a dream!

In the full sunshine pouring through the window, Meg's situation looked even more precarious than it had the previous night. She was no governess, and what would happen when the marquis discovered that fact?

She rested her head on her knees, letting her soft brown curls tumble about her face. How pleasant Brynwood seemed in comparison to living with the Barkers, and how free of the pressures which had pounded her from every side in London.

What would Lady Mary say? The thought reminded Meg that her mother and sister had planned an outing to Vauxhall the previous night. Had it come off? Had they been slighted? She wished she could know at once, and hoped they'd respond to her letter immediately.

Perhaps a note was already on its way from London to Derby, and she would miss it!

Indecisively Meg rose and dressed.

A thin-faced maid, whose name she believed was Bertha, knocked timidly. "Will you be taking breakfast with the children, miss?"

"Yes, that sounds like an excellent idea," Meg said.

She didn't fancy meeting his lordship again in her present state of mind. Already she was beginning to perceive the dangers inherent in living in the household of an attractive, unmarried man.

It might well be considered improper, even though the marquis didn't strike her as the type of blackguard to force his attentions on a lone female. Indeed, she couldn't imagine that he would need to *force* his presence on anyone. There was a magnetism about the man that showed itself in every move, in every expression on his handsome face....

Dear me, she told herself as she rose and went to the nursery. *I must guard my thoughts well. This man belongs to someone else.*

To Meg's relief, the sunny morning faces of Tom and Vanessa quickly drew her thoughts to more comfortable topics. Both were genuinely glad to see her, and although she doubted they were permanently reformed, at least it was apparent they had for the moment accepted her.

Meg was surprised how easily she slipped into her new role, teaching them to read in books which she found on the schoolroom shelves. The children were intelligent if undisciplined, and quickly applied themselves to their lessons. Even the rambunctious Vanessa kept her worst excesses under control, so long as Meg agreed to answer a question now and again about life in London and how a young lady went about becoming an Incomparable.

"I shall be a Diamond of the First Water!" declared the girl when they halted for luncheon.

"They won't let you go swimming in town!" protested her younger brother, misunderstanding the phrase. "Why would you want to do a thing like that, anyway?"

Vanessa rolled her eyes in disgust, and Meg laughed. "A Diamond of the First Water is a young lady who is highly regarded," she told Tom, "as I'm sure your sister will be, by all the gentlemen."

He wrinkled his nose. "Ugh. I shall never hang upon ladies. I shall be like Uncle Andrew and live here all by myself."

Meg merely smiled and handed him more bread and cheese.

The next few days passed with similar pleasantness. Lord Bryn remained a polite, dark shadow along the outskirts of their consciousness, only occasionally intruding himself upon the schoolroom.

Despite her resolve to push his lordship from her thoughts, Meg was aware of him always. Did he watch her, or was that only her imagination? If not, why did she feel a new sense of herself as a woman whenever he was near? Never before had she noticed the way her skirts swished when she turned, how artfully the bodice was sculpted across her bosom. Never before had her skin prickled this way, as if a feather were being run across it.

When she dared to observe the marquis directly, she noted a restlessness to his movements which reminded her of a caged creature. He seemed drawn to the schoolroom, where he watched the children with undisguised warmth. With Meg, he was more guarded, rarely meeting her gaze directly, yet from time to time he would take her elbow, or brush her shoulder as he moved past, small unintentional touches which seemed to fairly jolt through her.

At other moments, when the marquis thought himself unobserved, she would catch upon his face an expression of sorrow mingled with something else. A self-loathing? Had this anything to do with the Peninsula and the injury to his leg?

He was a many-faceted man, unlike the shallow pleasure-seeking bucks Meg had met in London. She could understand now why Lord Bryn avoided going to town. But there were other things about him beyond her understanding.

In spare moments, when the children were absorbed in their books, she wondered about Germaine Geraint. Friday-faced, Helen had called her, but a great gun, too. The marquis must care for her, if he planned to marry her. Such was the gossip even among the servants, for Miss Geraint and her parents were invited to visit in three weeks' time.

I hope she will suit him, Meg thought. *He deserves the best possible wife.*

She pushed away the thought that she could have been happy with such a man as this. For what did she really know of his soul? And if he had chosen Miss Geraint, surely it was from love. She was grateful for this chance to know him, and hence to know a little more about herself, and to grow closer to the children. At least she could find some happiness during this interlude, which was more than would have been possible in Derby.

On Friday Mrs. Franklin fetched Meg three letters from the village post. One, from her mother, expressed surprise and pleasure at the news that Meg was so well situated for the summer.

The second, from Helen, similarly conveyed good wishes, along with a piercing account of the rude behaviour of Lady Darnet at Vauxhall. It also announced that a garden party at the Cockerells' Kensington home would introduce Angela to society.

How typically generous of Helen! Meg thought as she turned to open the letter from her sister.

"Dearest Meg," Angela wrote, "Mother has explained to me the strictures of our finances. I hope you won't mind that we have made over your old dresses for me."

Mind indeed, silly goose! Meg thought. She read on, and was startled to learn of the conversation between Edward Cockerell and her sister at Vauxhall.

"I don't think he will tell anyone about your eyes," Angela wrote. "Pray forgive me, but I could not allow him to think so ill of you."

Stiff cheese. Meg remembered Helen's description of her brother, and laughed, picturing him confronted by the irascible Angela. The girl leaped readily to the defence of those she loved, and perhaps her doing so had proved fortunate. Else would Edward ever have agreed to the garden party?

She folded the letters away carefully. They would be answered that same night, and Meg regretted that she must tell lies. Well, at least she might invent two children for her imaginary friend—whom she had already described as married—and so draw upon the real antics of Tom and Vanessa.

She really should put a stop to this nonsense, she told herself. She should tell everyone the truth and go home. Perhaps at this juncture they would consider her action a mere eccentricity.

She had resolved to confront her employer on Saturday. However, that morning, as Meg and the children gathered for their reading, Lord Bryn strode into the schoolroom.

"There will be no lessons today," he declared. "We're going on a picnic."

Meg's spirits rose at once. She longed to see something of the countryside with the aid of her newly acquired lorgnette. Let the children have their fun, and that evening she would confide her errors to Lord Bryn.

A barouche awaited them in front of the house, its top folded down and a coachman perched in his high seat. The horses, Meg noted through the glass, were a perfectly matched pair of chestnuts.

"Shall we go to Marple?" Vanessa asked as her uncle handed her into the carriage. "I need new ribbons and laces."

"And emeralds and rubies?" inquired his lordship with a lift of the eyebrow. "Up you go, Tom."

"Can't I ride with Coachman?" demanded the little boy. "I want to take the reins!"

Meg laughed. "They've no scruples about asking for what they want, have they?" She laid her hand atop the marquis's as he assisted her, and wondered at the warmth which brightened her cheeks at his touch.

"I wouldn't call that asking." Lord Bryn climbed up to sit beside Tom and signalled Coachman to be off. "I would call that ordering, wouldn't you, Miss Linley?"

"Indeed." Meg placed a restraining hand on the bouncing Tom while informing Vanessa, "Ladies do not insist that gentlemen purchase items for them."

"He's not a gentleman! He's Uncle Andrew!" was the reply, at which the adults exchanged amused glances.

It was a splendid day for an outing, and Meg revelled in the newfound privilege of being able to see her surroundings. Each tree and cloud, each flower and bird was a marvellous discovery. To Meg, the barouche travelled through a wonderful landscape, filled with previously unsuspected details and hues.

"You take an unusual interest in the scenery," observed the marquis.

His deep voice rumbled through Meg's bones, nearly unnerving her. Whyever was she reacting in this childish manner? Doing her best to retain her composure, she said, "As I have explained, I cannot see well, and this quizzing glass has opened a new world to me."

"Indeed?" His lordship frowned. "I had thought the thing merely an affectation."

He reached across and lifted the lorgnette to his own eye. As Meg had tied it about her neck by a long black velvet ribbon for fear of losing it, this required that she lean toward him.

Bryn removed the glass quickly. "Maddening," he said. "It distorts."

"Does it?" said Meg, straightening. "I believe it corrects distortion if any exists."

His lordship regarded her thoughtfully, taking advantage of the children's absorption in spying rabbits among the tufts of grass. "What is your age, Miss Linley?"

Meg knew she was much too young to be a governess, but she would not give him a direct lie. "Nineteen, my lord," she said.

"Nineteen?" The marquis stared in disbelief. "Whatever can Standish have been thinking of?"

Meg swallowed, taking the opportunity to say, "I fear there has been some misunderstanding. You see..."

"A fox!" Vanessa jumped to her feet. "Look, right there!"

As she spoke, a small, red-coated animal darted almost beneath the hooves of the horses, which shied. The young girl would have been tossed into the road and perhaps severely injured but for the speed with which her uncle seized her.

Amid Vanessa's squeals and Tom's yells, the barouche jerked to a halt.

"Oh, my!" the girl gasped. "Please let me get down. Look, my legs are trembling! Tom, can you see that?" She raised her skirt, curiosity overwhelming any trace of modesty.

"You call that trembling?" snorted Tom. "When I had the fever last winter, I shivered so much the bed shook."

"Pooh! You're making that up!"

"I think we shall eat our luncheon here," remarked the marquis calmly.

"Vanessa, you must never stand up in an open carriage again!" scolded Meg as they descended to the ground. Despite the children's nonsensical argument, her heart still thudded loudly.

"I shan't, Miss Linley. But wasn't I trembling mightily?" The child bounced to the ground, and Meg could see the lesson was already forgotten.

Coachman spread out a blanket for them beside a stream, where overhanging trees blocked the midday sun's heat. The driver took himself off, having been provided with his own lunch.

In the basket Cook had prepared, Meg found cold chicken, fruit, wine and peach tarts. Before eating, the children raced each other up and back along the waterway, but afterward, with their stomachs full, they lay on the grass and dozed.

"How peaceful they look," Meg observed. The domesticity of the scene reawakened her longing for a family of her own, and brought with it a stab of pain.

"You are very good with them, despite your youth, Miss Linley," said the marquis.

She smiled, her blue eyes meeting his brown ones in shared affection for the youngsters. Here was an opportunity to confide the truth to him. Meg swallowed hard against a sudden nervousness. "Do you remember what I told you when I arrived?"

He thought for a moment. "No, I'm afraid I do not."

"That tale of being a lady who had mistaken your carriage for a post chaise?" she prompted.

"Ah." A smile warmed the darkness of his eyes. "Yes, indeed I do."

"Suppose it were true?" Meg asked. "Suppose I were not a governess at all, but, well, someone of good family."

"Are you flirting with me, Miss Linley?" he asked with mock sternness.

She blushed. "I didn't intend it, my lord."

"No, I'm sure you didn't." To her confusion he reached over and lifted her hand, turning it in his and examining the palm. "A delicate hand. What is your real story, Miss Linley? Were you orphaned, perhaps?"

"My father died when I was young," she admitted, "and my mother has fallen upon hard times. There is a younger sister whom I dearly love, and hope to see well married."

"But not yourself?" He retained her hand in his.

"Me?" Meg feigned lightness of spirit. "Oh, perhaps when I am older."

"You like children." It was not a question but a statement. "And you are quite fetching, my dear, if you will forgive my boldness. I cannot imagine why you should have chosen to take this post so far from town."

"Nor can I," she said. "It was not precisely a decision so much as a . . . an accident, my lord."

"Selecting the wrong carriage?" he teased. His face was very near.

"Yes," she whispered. "I had meant to tell you. . . ."

His lips grazed hers, ever so softly. "Forgive the liberty," he murmured, still without releasing her hand. "I know you're a respectable young woman, Miss Linley, but you're the first person I've met in two years, aside from the children, who can make me forget what happened."

Meg knew she shouldn't be sitting here, shouldn't have permitted the highly improper kiss, but her mouth would not speak and her knees would not obey. She could neither stand nor protest, only sit gazing mutely into the pain that hid behind his eyes.

I could love such a man, she thought.

As for Lord Bryn, he found himself in a quandary. Until the past few days, he had imagined his life neatly pigeonholed and his future guarded against any unwanted emotion.

There would be a marriage to Miss Geraint, or if she refused, to someone else with the same uncomplicated nature. The lady might spend part of her year in London, if she wished; there would be separate bedchambers, of course, except for the time needed to produce an heir.

Not that Lord Bryn lacked the customary urges of a young man, but he had long ago learned to suppress them. To allow anyone to become close was to expose himself to even more pain, and to risk losing what little remained of his pride.

Now danger had come from an unforeseen quarter. He needed a governess for the children and had been delighted to find Miss Linley so well adapted. But now...

His conduct today was highly unorthodox and objectionable. The woman should have slapped his face after that kiss. Did she fear losing her position and being turned away without references? He would never forgive himself if he were taking advantage of her vulnerability. But in her gentle eyes he saw no unhappiness, only warmth.

Did she feel as he did? Or was he mistaken, and this Miss Linley a woman of dubious character? In any event, she was surely unsuitable to be his wife. How then could he nurse such tender feelings for her?

Disturbed by his own reflections, the marquis jumped to his feet and began to stroll along the bank, pretending to study the patterns of ripples and the silver swirl of fish. He should send her away. But on what pretext? The children would be horrified, though Miss Linley might have just reason to wish herself away.

No, there must be some better solution. If, for example, she were to marry.

Andrew did not like that prospect, but he had to concede that it was an excellent idea, and would serve both his purposes and the children's. If Miss Linley were to marry someone who lived in the neighbourhood, she might continue to work here on a daily basis without risk to her character. Under such circumstances, the marquis concluded, she would be protected against her own weakness, and more to the point, his.

"Miss Linley." He returned to sit beside the young woman, who appeared perplexed. He had not meant to leave her so abruptly, but he had needed time to sort his thoughts.

"Yes, my lord?"

"There is an entertainment planned for tonight at the home of Squire Roberts, who owns the estate that marches with mine," said Lord Bryn, who until this moment had intended to send the squire his regrets. "The invitation was meant to include my household, and as you are now a part of it, I thought you might enjoy making new acquaintances."

A troubled expression crossed the young woman's face.

"You need not go, of course, if you do not wish it," he hurried to add.

"The people who will attend all live hereabouts?" asked Miss Linley. "They are not from London, by any chance?"

"No," he replied, puzzled.

"I...as I believe I mentioned, my family has come down in the world, and I wouldn't wish the embarrassment of encountering some old acquaintance," she explained. "But since that isn't likely to occur, I'm pleased to accept your generous offer."

Lord Bryn smiled warmly at the prospect of the coming evening. They might even dance together, although not more than once. But it would be enough to hold her in his arms and whirl her gently through a waltz.

Then he remembered that the object of this exercise was to find Miss Linley a suitable husband. Damnation! The fellow had better appreciate her, or he would have to answer to Andrew Davis.

"Coachman!" called his lordship, his loud voice awakening the children. "It's time to go home!"

CHAPTER EIGHT

THE SOCIETY in northeast Cheshire was sharply limited by the size of the population and by the region's remoteness. However enchanting the black-and-white magpie houses and the wild moors might be, they could not adequately replace ladies wearing fashions copied from the French and gentlemen dressed to outdo the Beau.

Or so any member of the elite would have said.

Curiously, the residents of Marple, Stockport, and vicinity remained unaware that they were deficient in any regard. They believed talk of Wellington and Napoleon, of farming conditions, and of trouble over industrialization in the North to be an adequate replacement for gossip and rumour, although they also knew how to amuse themselves in dancing and cards.

In these parts it was considered that if a lady possessed intelligent conversation, a warm heart, or a talent for the domestic arts, she might be an excellent candidate for matrimony despite a thick ankle, unfashionable clothing—or weak eyes.

And so it was, at the solid home of Esquire Roberts, that Meg Linley found herself for the first time an object of approval and even admiration.

The Alton sisters, both approaching their late seventies, commented favourably on her bell-like voice. Mrs. Albert Ludden, wife of the curate, remarked upon the excellence of Miss Linley's manners, while her plain daughter, Veronica, stared at the newcomer with something approaching awe. Squire Roberts, who had been seeking a second wife since the death of his first several years earlier, found Meg thoroughly enchanting, even to the gleaming facets of her lorgnette.

As Mrs. Ludden played the pianoforte, Meg joined the assembly in a set of country dances, and then, her breath recovered, sang with them. What a pleasure to read the words upon the page through her eyeglass instead of mouthing empty syllables! Her pleasant soft soprano blended effortlessly with the marquis's rumbling baritone.

"'Tis rare good fortune to find such a pearl newly arrived in our region," the host declared when they had finished, pressing a glass of ratafia upon Meg. He was a man of middle years, stocky in build, with a face that might once have been handsome but now showed traces of excessive use of alcohol.

"I've never felt more welcome anywhere," Meg said truthfully. "The good fortune is mine."

She allowed the squire to introduce her to his eldest son, Jeffrey, who at two and twenty was a strapping lad with a solid, dependable way about him.

"Not much younger'n you, Miss, I daresay, for all you've need of a quizzing glass," joked the squire. Meg smiled and held her tongue.

She noted Lord Bryn regarding her with a curious expression, as if she'd done something mildly displeasing. Meg searched her memory for some misdeed but found none. Perhaps it was the simplicity of her dress, a blue muslin which she had considered flattering to her eyes; it was the most elegant of the gowns she had brought.

Confused, Meg retreated to the rooms set aside for ladies, where a maid helped restore an errant curl. A moment later, a large girl entered, whom Meg recognized as Veronica Ludden, the curate's daughter.

The younger woman sank into a chair beside Meg, a look of envy on her freckled face. Not a displeasing countenance, Meg decided, although the girl moved awkwardly, as if she had only just been introduced to her knees and elbows.

"You've spent most of your life in London, haven't you?" asked Veronica without preamble.

"No, only the past few years," Meg said. "Why do you ask?"

A shrug. "Only that...one can see just by looking that you always know the right thing to do."

This observation struck Meg dumb with astonishment. She, Meg Linley, the great gawk, suddenly become an arbiter of manners? The suggestion was highly amusing, but she took pains to hide her reaction from the earnest Miss Ludden.

"That's very kind, but I'm afraid I don't deserve such a compliment," Meg said.

Veronica regarded her in the mirror. "You met him, didn't you?"

"Who?"

"Jeffrey."

Ah. The reverential tone with which the name was uttered told everything.

"Is he your beau?" Meg ventured.

Veronica shook her head ruefully. "If I knew how to go on as you do... But my father doesn't hold with fripperies. He's the curate, you know. I'm not to have deportment lessons, and my mother's made-over dresses are good enough for me." She gestured down at the heavy chintz gown she wore, in a style ten years out of date.

"How old are you?" Meg asked.

"Seventeen."

She would have guessed Veronica to be her elder by several years, and this disclosure wrenched at Meg's heart.

"It's not difficult," Meg said, although she doubted a moment's conversation would be of much help. "You must move with grace, as if...as if you might fly at any moment, but delicately, like a swan."

Oh, how the ton would laugh to hear her speak so, she reflected. But in truth, with her lorgnette, Meg could step out with as much confidence as anyone.

"Like this?" To the amazement of the maid, Veronica stood up and glided across the floor.

"That's the idea," Meg said encouragingly. "But you must keep your shoulders straight, and not thrust your neck forward. The point is not to imitate a swan, but to capture the spirit of one."

Veronica turned and, following instructions, performed a creditable sweep across the room.

"Yes!" said Meg. "You have a natural talent for it, I believe."

The younger girl beamed. "Do you really think so?" Then her expression sobered. "But it's entirely different when I try to speak to Jeffrey. I don't know how to do it."

Meg had never given much thought to such matters, having been more concerned with avoiding crashes into serving maids and stumbles over the furniture. Now she tried to recall the natural way she responded to the marquis, for he was the only gentleman whom she could recall truly liking.

"You must gaze directly into his eyes without fidgeting," she instructed. "Smile, but not too broadly, and pay close attention to what he says."

"That's all very well, but sometimes I must speak also!" protested Veronica, crossing her arms in front of her chest.

"There!" Meg pointed. "That is not swanlike."

Veronica uncrossed the arms and clasped her hands in a more becoming fashion.

"Much better," said Meg, unconsciously assuming her governess voice. "Now, when you speak to him, you should answer his questions honestly but briefly, and in return ask him whatever you wish to know. So long as it isn't improper, of course," she added quickly.

Veronica sighed. "Perhaps if I were to watch you talk with someone you liked, I would understand better."

Meg had no intention of flirting with the marquis under the noses of his neighbours. What a bit of tittle-tattle that would make! But the kindly squire might be flattered by her attentions, as men of advancing years often were with young women.

"Very well," she said. "I will demonstrate upon the father, and you shall follow suit with the son."

"Oh, Miss Linley!" Veronica clapped her hands together. "You are a great sport!"

Smiling, the two women returned to the company. Meg was pleased to think that she might help another young woman enter society, as Helen had so often helped her.

Her task was made easier by the sudden appearance of Squire Roberts at her side. "Are you a horsewoman, Miss Linley?"

Conscious of Veronica's gaze upon her, Meg turned slightly toward him and stared directly up into his watery eyes. "Why, no, I fear not. My poor vision has prevented it."

"Demmed shame." The fellow glowed under her attentions. "Got a new hunter to try out this fall. Should have a rousing season. Countryside's teeming with foxes."

Meg recalled the small red creature which had nearly caused Vanessa's downfall in the carriage. "So I've observed," she agreed, placing one hand lightly on the squire's arm. "Another time, perhaps I may see your new horse. I'm sure he's splendid."

A glance over her shoulder revealed a touching tableau.

Veronica Ludden had fluttered across the room, to the amazement of her mother, and alit at the elbow of Jeffrey

Roberts. The young man was at that moment engaged in conversation with the Misses Alton's grandniece, a fetching young girl with russet hair and grey eyes.

"I hope you're enjoying your stay in these parts," Jeffrey was saying to Miss Conley when he felt an arm slip through his and turned in astonishment to see the curate's ungainly daughter.

"Yes, I do most sincerely hope so," agreed Veronica, as if it were the most natural thing in the world for her to stand here at Jeffrey's side. "How long will you be staying?"

In his shock, he could think of no polite way to disentangle himself from the ensuing chatter. As for Veronica, she was astonished at her own daring and could attribute it only to Miss Linley's example. From time to time, the girl stole glances at the more accomplished woman, and imitated her as closely as possible.

Well aware that she was under scrutiny, Meg dimpled prettily when the squire offered to fetch her another glass of ratafia, although in truth she hated the sweet cordial and would have much preferred a cup of tea.

With the aid of the lorgnette, she noted something she would never have seen otherwise, that the marquis was regarding her with a deepening frown. Surely the simplicity of her dress could not provoke him to that extent. Did he regret his impulse in bringing her this evening? Meg wondered. He might think a governess out of place among these gentlefolk. Well, he could scarcely blame her for his own invitation!

Across the room, Mrs. Ludden resumed her seat at the piano and began to play. Jeffrey, seeing his chance for escape, asked the enchanting Miss Conley to dance.

Veronica suffered pangs of humiliation, painfully aware that she was standing with her arm tucked through Jeffrey's even as he flirted with this interloper.

She glanced nervously at Meg. However, unlike his son, the squire gave no sign of turning his attentions to any rival lady. Deprived of a model, the curate's daughter yielded reluctantly, saying only, "How kind of you to make Miss Conley feel welcome, Jeffrey."

Blushing fiercely under the disapproving eye of her father, who had taken in this curious scene, Veronica hastened to Meg's side as the squire departed to retrieve the ratafia.

"Now what am I to do?" she cried. "He's much taken with that Conley girl, and I'm not half so pretty as she!"

Meg pressed her lips together reflectively. "He cannot properly dance with her twice in succession. When they're finished, walk up to them and make some proprietary remark which will obligate him to ask you next."

The girl didn't look entirely convinced. The squire returned then, and Meg seized the opportunity. "I hadn't realized, sir, when I accepted the ratafia that we should be treated to more music. I noted before what an excellent dancer you are."

"Did you?" A broad grin revealed a set of teeth as square-shaped as the squire himself. "Would you honour me with this dance, Miss Linley?"

Veronica nodded as she watched them walk away. No sooner had the music ended than she approached Jeffrey. "Isn't he a superb dancer?" she said to Miss Conley, slipping her arm once again through that of her prey.

Mrs. Ludden struck up a new dance, and Jeffrey was obligated to turn to this annoying companion and invite her to be his partner. Only after she accepted did he realize the music was a waltz. Swallowing his apprehensions, for Veronica Ludden had rendered more than one gentleman temporarily crippled upon the dance floor, Jeffrey took her in his arms.

To his surprise, she moved gracefully, smiled warmly up at him, and made tinkling, bright conversation instead of staring cow-eyed and speechless in her usual manner.

"You are much changed, Miss Ludden," he observed. "Have you been taking lessons?"

"Lessons?"

"In dancing." What else could he have meant? he wondered.

"Yes. No. Well, not precisely." Veronica glanced nervously at her father glowering by the pianoforte, but forged ahead bravely. "I'm determined to transform myself into a young lady." Then came her stroke of inspiration. She added in a conspiratorial tone, "Would you be so kind as to help me?"

"In what way?" he asked, guiding her past his father and Miss Linley.

"I fear I'm terribly awkward." Veronica could feel the change in him, the surge of sympathy which showed as his eyes met hers. "Miss Conley is so beautiful, but of course she's had opportunities, which I have not, to go about in society and meet young gentlemen."

"You're not so inelegant as you fear." It was the strongest compliment he could honestly tender.

"Yes but ... if you could spare me a bit of your time, at such events as these, to help me improve my manner, I should be ever so grateful."

What gentleman could resist so complimentary a request? "Of course, I shall do my best," he said.

From that moment on, Veronica became Jeffrey's protégée, and for the rest of the evening he regarded her with new eyes. He saw not her faults but every small improvement, and paid her the bulk of his attention, to the mystification of Miss Conley.

As for Meg, she was finding the squire more pressing in his attentions than she cared for, or had expected. "Will you not come and see my rose garden?'' he asked when they had finished a waltz.

"At night?'' countered Meg, restraining the urge to rub her foot where he had stepped on it.

"Ah, indeed, 'tis dark.'' Squire Roberts stared at the window accusingly, as if the sky had darkened purposely to thwart him. "The orangerie, then? I have a lemon tree all in bloom.''

The image of the heavy, phlegmatic squire framed by the delicate blossoms of a lemon tree struck Meg as humorous, and she began to laugh.

"I say!'' The man wasn't sure how to respond.

"Pray forgive me.'' She controlled her mirth. "It's only that one thinks of lemons as sour, and I cannot imagine one in bloom!'' It was the only excuse to come to mind, and a weak one at that. In fact she had seen such trees in London and loved the rich fragrance.

The marquis approached and said coldly, "I believe we should be going, Miss Linley, if we are to arise in time for church in the morning.''

"Of course.'' She excused herself from the squire's company with barely disguised relief.

After a ripple of farewells, Meg found herself being handed up into the curricle by his lordship. Taking his place beside her, he lifted the reins and slapped them against the horses' backs.

The night was warm and they rode for a time without speaking. Meg gazed up through the lorgnette, marvelling at the beauty of the heretofore invisible stars.

The silence weighed on her, however, and she wondered if she should speak. She hesitated to invite trouble by asking the marquis what had overset him, and yet she couldn't bear to go on wondering.

"Have I given offence, my lord?'' she asked at last.

"Offence?" The indifference in his tone was feigned, she felt certain.

"Perhaps it is my gown," Meg ventured. "It's the best I possess, but I fear not so fine as those of some of the ladies."

"Your gown? No, I have no complaint. And if I had, I should blame myself for not paying you a better wage," said the marquis. The curricle rolled on through the night amid the soft, familiar noises of hooves thumping against dirt and leather harnesses creaking.

The man was being impossible! Meg glared at him, but he presented a frozen profile. A very handsome profile, she conceded, with high cheekbones and a sharp nose. It bespoke character, Lady Mary would have said.

At the thought of her mother, Meg felt a pang of homesickness. What were they doing tonight? Which gown would Angela wear to the garden party? How would the ton respond to her?

If only she could be there, Meg wished heartily. But how was she to take her leave? After that kiss in the countryside, how could she confess the truth to Lord Bryn?

"Am I correct in assuming that you do not wish to remain a governess for long?" enquired the marquis icily.

Fear flashed over Meg. "I beg your pardon?"

"From your conduct with Squire Roberts, I take it that you have some interest in that regard," he said.

"Interest?" She stared at Lord Bryn in amazement. Did he believe that she had set her cap for Squire Roberts?

"Or is it your custom to flirt boldly with whatever gentleman seeks you out?" he pursued relentlessly.

"I—" Meg stopped. She had been about to protest that she didn't mean to flirt, but that wasn't true. Nor could she explain that her conduct had been a demonstration for Veronica; that would require violating a confidence, which she would not do.

"How you conduct yourself with men of your own acquaintance is none of my affair," his lordship continued, "but when you behave with such...shameless abandon, under my very nose, I cannot but remark upon it."

"Shameless abandon!" Meg sat up angrily. "My lord, I realize that as my employer you may say what you wish—"

"Oh, I don't stand on privilege," he snapped, his eyes still fixed on the moonlit path before them. "You may reply however you wish without fear of losing your references, Miss Linley."

"What have I done to merit such an accusation?" she demanded. "Danced with the squire once—"

"A waltz," he pointed out tersely.

"Accepted a glass of ratafia—"

"Two," he said.

"Spoke with him privately for a moment—"

"Placed your hand on his arm," the marquis corrected.

"And refused his invitation to stroll in his rose garden," she finished. "Or smell his lemon tree." At the memory, she began to laugh all over again.

"I fail to see the humour." Lord Bryn guided the team around a pothole.

"Pardon me." She chuckled. "It was only that I imagined Squire Roberts standing solidly beneath one of those airy little trees, doing his best to look poetic and succeeding only in looking entirely absurd!"

At this outburst, the marquis's visage softened. "You don't take him seriously?"

"Not in the least," Meg affirmed.

His lordship clucked to the horses. "Then I have made a cake of myself, haven't I?"

"No, you haven't," Meg assured him, although she was puzzled by this conduct. Had she not known of his lordship's feelings for Germaine Geraint, she might almost have supposed him to be jealous. "If I offended propriety, you were right to rebuke me. But I assure you, it's only that I don't know the customs in this region."

"You did not offend propriety," said the marquis. "I'm merely in a bad temper. It was hot today, and we've been short of rain this summer. I'm concerned about my tenants."

As they rode the rest of the way back to Brynwood in a more companionable silence, he wondered why he had criticized the governess. It had been his object to find Miss Linley a husband. Why then should he be so irritated to see her dance in the arms of that aging Romeo?

Surely it was paternal concern for a valued governess, he told himself. The late Mrs. Roberts had been a timid woman, cowed by a bullying husband, and despite his charming manners tonight, the squire was known to be a rough man when crossed.

That was reason enough for his concern, the marquis decided.

He glanced at Meg, riding dreamily alongside him. What was she thinking? Emotions played across her face, soft and intriguing. One might almost guess that she was reliving the evening, waltzing again with the squire. Or was she recalling the first set of country dances which she had performed with Bryn himself?

The marquis wished he knew more of her. A careful review of Standish's note had revealed little. Excellent references, but how long could she have been working if she was only nineteen?

He had behaved very badly this evening, Bryn reflected unhappily. How frightened she'd looked when he made that remark about her wishing to leave her post, as if she thought he would dismiss her! Would he never learn to think of anyone but himself? he wondered. He dreaded someday causing injury to another as he had to Harry, through his own selfish disregard.

As they passed from one shadow to the next beneath the three-quarter moon, the marquis reflected for the first time that perhaps he despised London society not so much because of the frailties of others but because of his own. How easily he might slip into gaming, into attending the sales at Tattersall's, visiting his tailor, dining at his club, and never sparing a thought for anyone else.

Here in the country, one lived close to one's subordinates. The marquis kept a watchful eye on his tenants, making certain they were adequately provided for and discreetly aided when illness struck. He cherished his two little wards, and strove to deal fairly with his servants.

Why then did Miss Linley knock asunder his best intentions? He had been prepared to quarrel with her tonight, to cast her in the worst possible light, when she had only behaved as any young lady might in the presence of a marriageable gentleman.

A marriageable gentleman? That bounder Roberts! If the chap ever laid one hand on Miss Linley, the marquis would call him out!

Astounded at the ferocity of his sentiments, Lord Bryn spent the rest of the ride home paying close attention to the horses.

CHAPTER NINE

"I CANNOT THINK why I let you talk me into coming," said Lady Darnet, adjusting her chip straw bonnet as the landau carried her and her cousin Sir Manfred along Kensington Road.

She glanced out at the vegetable-laden carts and pedestrian fruit-sellers heading in the opposite direction, for Kensington provided much of London's produce. With annoyance, she noted how her carriage was forced to slow as it made its way through the throngs of girls with their baskets of cherries, apricots, and strawberries. It was not the countess's nature to concern herself if a child stumbled beneath a heavy load or wept over the spilled contents of a basket. She simply despised obstacles.

Her rotund companion shrugged. "I thought you might enjoy the outing, dear cousin," he said. "And the events of the day may prove amusing. One talks of nothing else at White's."

"One must be excessively dull then, I should think," Cynthia retorted.

She hadn't recovered from her pique the previous Tuesday at seeing that Linley creature making up to Mr. Cockerell. Having married once for money, Cynthia fully intended to claim herself a handsome young man this time, and Edward Cockerell met her requirements.

Indeed, in his admiring glances and increasingly frequent visits to her home, the young man had shown every sign of offering for her. His tardiness in doing so she attributed to the reluctance of a longtime bachelor to relinquish his single state, and so had determined to encourage his suit with some strategy of her own.

She had been on the point of speaking to him at Vauxhall, in hopes of arousing his jealousy toward her elderly companion, when the Linleys cut off her approach. Why had he permitted them to join his family?

Cynthia wished she knew what he and the chit had been discussing so earnestly after the quadrille, and why he was sponsoring this ill-advised come-out party.

Perhaps she had been wrong about him, Cynthia mused. He might not be suitable as a husband. But no. She had watched him covertly for years, even before her aging spouse stuck his spoon in the wall, and this was the first time Mr. Cockerell had made a serious blunder.

It might well have resulted from the influence of his unruly sister. She posed a special sort of problem, for Cynthia could hardly slight Helen and hope to retain the attentions of the brother. Best to concentrate on discouraging the Linley girl.

"A fellow can't help noticing she's a taking little thing, that Angela," noted her cousin, oblivious to the countess's mood. "Such big blue eyes!"

Big blue eyes indeed! How common they looked, Cynthia thought, silently congratulating herself on the subtle elegance of her own grey ones.

Yet she well knew the advantage eighteen has over seven and twenty in the freshness of youth and the soundness of constitution. She herself nursed a toothache at the back of her mouth and feared the tooth soon must be replaced by a china one from Wedgwood. Nor could even the whiteness lent by a Spanish paper entirely disguise the roughening of her delicate skin by harsh cosmetics.

"I was dancing with the elder Miss Linley that very evening at Almack's," Sir Manfred remarked as the carriage turned onto Kensington High Street. "Didn't snub *me*. Can't say why she took it into her head to cut Brummell."

"You don't suppose he'll be attending today?" asked Cynthia with a spark of interest.

Her cousin shook his head. "He's out of town, and so is Prinny, but I warrant the Cockerells'll not lack for amusing guests all the same."

The Cockerells' second home was located between Kensington Palace and Holland House, the turreted Jacobean mansion where Whig statesmen, scholars, writers, and wits gathered. Cynthia had wished to see the affair poorly attended, but her hopes were dashed by the crush of carriages approaching the location.

"What? Not Lady Jersey!" she declared on recognizing a coat of arms.

"One could hardly keep her away from an event which is on every tongue," said Sir Manfred. "And this business of being sponsored by the Cockerells, suppose the chit turns out to be the Incomparable of the season? Sally Jersey will want to see for herself."

Cynthia sniffed. "I can't imagine that the Linleys will be granted any more vouchers to Almack's."

Her resentment of Angela Linley derived from more than ordinary jealousy. Despite her marriage, Cynthia's ancestry contained its share of dubious elements, among them a grandmother who had married her own coachman. With such questionable relations, she felt herself ill-placed beside a young lady whose grandfathers had been, respectively, a viscount and an earl. Therefore she begrudged Angela any small advantage in their mutual quest, as she saw it, to bring Edward Cockerell up to scratch.

The gentleman in question was, at that moment, seriously questioning his own sanity as he greeted yet another of the hundreds of guests who thronged the garden.

One couldn't deny the beauty of the setting, with its luxurious flower beds, delightfully secluded arbours, and climbing roses. But he knew full well that the cream of the ton had not driven to Kensington to admire the flora. The object of their attention was standing beside her mother, smiling demurely and looking like an exquisite flower in a gown of silver, threaded with pink ribbons.

The dress itself offended him. Why hadn't she worn the conventional white? Why had she chosen a costume, however discreet, that flattered her complexion so outrageously and called undue attention to her beauty? Far more seemly to have retreated into the obscurity of plainness until that business of her sister was forgotten.

Edward's temper was only mildly improved by his observing the entrance of Lady Darnet with her cousin, the baronet. She looked as exquisite as ever, but... Did she always have that look of coolness about the eyes? And perhaps it was the direct sunlight, but he remarked a roughness of her skin which had previously escaped his notice.

"My dear countess." He bent over her hand. "Without you, our day would have been sadly incomplete."

"Naturally I couldn't absent myself from this lovely entertainment," she replied graciously. "You know Sir Manfred, I believe?"

The two men nodded to each other.

Helen approached and extended her own welcome to Lady Darnet, but there was no warmth in it. Edward tried to catch his sister's eye with a warning glare, but she ignored him. One would almost think the chit wanted to ruin his suit!

"You will save me a dance, I trust?" he asked the countess. "We are to have dancing out of doors. A special floor has been laid for it."

"I would be delighted." She smiled, allowing her gaze to meet his and hold it for a moment. What a relief to discover that his heart had not been won away, although in truth the heart was an organ for which Cynthia Darnet had little use.

"Oh, pooh," said Helen when the countess and her cousin had moved away. "You're not still dangling after her, are you, Edward?"

The coldness of his answering stare would have chilled a less bold spirit. "If you cannot behave with propriety, Helen, perhaps we should retire to Somerset," he said.

"Sometimes I should think you nine and sixty instead of nine and twenty," retorted his sister. Before he could reply, she turned to greet the latest arrivals.

Angela, standing nearby beside her mother, had caught some of this conversation. Why did it disturb her that Mr. Cockerell was enamoured of the undeniably beautiful Lady Darnet? And that he had regarded Angela herself with such distaste this afternoon?

"Do you think my dress is wrong?" she whispered to her mother. "Would white have been better?"

Lady Mary didn't reply. Unfortunately Meg's white come-out gown had failed to survive an encounter with a drunken gentleman's supper plate the previous year. To maintain their rented house until August would require the most stringent of economies, and in the absence of a formal ball, a white dress was not strictly necessary. So the silver, artfully trimmed with new ribbons, must serve instead. Lady Mary knew as well as anyone that this fête's popularity derived from curiosity rather than respect. One could only hope that Angela's lovely freshness would overcome the doubters.

Gradually the gardens filled with guests, gaily dressed in springtime colours. The small orchestra wafted a charming melody across the lawn, and couples began to dance beneath a striped canopy on the specially laid oak floor.

"You look beautiful." Helen slipped her arm through Angela's. "Come and dance with Edward."

"Oh, that's not necessary...."

The hostess refused to listen. To her embarrassment, Angela found herself thrust upon the obviously unhappy gentleman.

"Behave yourself, Edward!" Helen said by way of a parting reminder. "Remember, you are the host."

"I must apologize," Angela said as she and Edward strolled toward the pole-supported canopy, which had been left open to a height of six feet. "You have been most gracious about this affair, and I promise to restrain Helen if in future she tries to force you to attend on me."

Something about this speech touched Edward—perhaps the self-effacing manner in which it was delivered, or the genuine note of apology in that young face.

"I recognize that this is none of your doing," he said. "And I have already acknowledged you to be the victim of innocent mischance, where your sister is concerned." It was as far as he was willing to venture toward peacemaking, but at least they were not at sword's point when they stepped out to perform a stately pavane.

Watching from the side, the countess snapped open her fan and fluttered it angrily. Was the man declaring his intentions? Why had he requested a dance of Cynthia earlier if he meant to expend his flatteries on this milk-and-water miss?

She consented tersely to dance with her cousin and made a point of ignoring the other couple. Why did Edward smile down at the chit? How could he succumb to a girl who would wear silver at her own come-out?

Lady Darnet's irritation grew as she danced with one gentleman after another, and none of them Mr. Cockerell. Her sore tooth only added to her mounting outrage. How dare he slight her in this fashion? She knew her own worth, as a countess and as heiress to her late husband's fortune! The Cockerells were highly placed, but not so highly as she.

To make matters worse, the other guests appeared to be enjoying themselves. After the initial inquisitiveness wore itself thin, the brightness of the day invaded their spirits, and they all but forgot their reason for attending.

Even Sally Jersey condescended to speak to Lady Mary, congratulating her on the success of her younger daughter. She added, loudly enough for others to hear, that Brummell had said he believed, after reading the elder Miss Linley's apology, that she had been wool-gathering at Almack's. Therefore her slight, while a serious breach of conduct, might not be entirely unforgivable.

It was enough to give one the megrim!

By the time Edward Cockerell freed himself from his duties and approached Lady Darnet, her mood hovered dangerously on the brink of fury. Nevertheless, she managed to curtsey and nod pleasantly. He had no notion that her habitually cool demeanour hid a violent temper, and the countess didn't intend to make that fact apparent at this point in the game.

The musicians began a waltz. Not only could she hold Edward in her arms, Cynthia reflected cheerfully, but Angela must stand aside entirely, having not yet received permission from the patronesses to perform this intimate dance.

Except that Lady Jersey, the leading patroness, was smiling and nodding at some request of Sir Manfred's. And now he was strolling across to Angela and leading her onto the floor.

Betrayed by her own cousin! Cynthia could have screamed with frustration.

"You seem perturbed, Lady Darnet," said Mr. Cockerell, his hand at her waist as they swayed in time to the music. "Have I said something amiss?"

Cynthia managed a practised smile, despite the nagging toothache. "Why, no, of course not." Her voice tinkled in the warm air. "Such nonsense, Mr. Cockerell! You are always the soul of propriety!"

"So I should like to think." He looked pleased. What a handsome man he was, large enough to top her own tall figure but graceful and slim nonetheless. And this Kensington estate, as well as the one in Somerset and the London town house... Yes, Lady Darnet would enjoy being their mistress.

"I must say it was kind of you to bring out Miss Angela," she murmured. "Poor little soul. She does need one's charity."

"Oh?" He frowned. "Forgive me, Lady Darnet, but I noted at Vauxhall that you avoided her company. Had she given you offence?"

Dash him! Cynthia clenched her jaw. Oh! Her tooth! It took a great effort of will to reply sweetly, "You must have mistaken my intentions, sir. I would never have slighted the girl. Indeed, I am sure I did not notice her."

"Of course," he replied.

Was he defending the sprig? Lady Darnet's eyes narrowed. She would not allow herself to be put in an awkward light. Why had everyone here forgotten so quickly about the Linleys' disgrace?

The waltz ended, and Cynthia and Edward joined a small cluster of people about the refreshment table. Here were Sir Manfred and Angela, Lady Jersey, a woman whom Cynthia identified as Mr. Cockerell's Aunt Emily, and several others of their acquaintance.

Well, if they had forgotten the Linleys' fall from grace, she would remind them.

Accepting a glass of orangeat, Cynthia observed in dulcet tones, "How unfortunate that Mr. Brummell could not attend." A shocked silence greeted this remark, and she added swiftly, "His presence does always grace an assembly, don't you think so, madam?"

The target of her question, Mr. Cockerell's aunt, fixed Cynthia with a cold stare. "Grandson of a valet!" she sniffed.

The countess gasped and turned to Lady Jersey for support. "But he *is* Prinny's friend!"

"Indeed." The mistress of London society remained noncommittal, too fascinated by this exchange to end it.

"His presence might have been awkward," ventured Sir Manfred, grinning foolishly at the silent Angela. "I think he means to make his peace with the Linleys, once the dust has settled."

This conversation wasn't going at all the way Cynthia intended. She peeked at Mr. Cockerell and saw a dark look upon his visage as he gazed at the girl in silver. Well, he at least shared her sentiment!

"I should hardly take a gentleman's absence as indication of his goodwill," she replied.

The response, in a mutter almost too low to make out, came once again from Mr. Cockerell's aunt. "Granddaughter of a coachman," she growled.

Cynthia paled and her hand flew to her cheek, inadvertently striking the very tooth that troubled her. With a cry of mingled fury and pain, she rushed away.

Sir Manfred and Mr. Cockerell hurried after her. "Pray forgive my aunt," said the young man. "She speaks her thoughts aloud without considering their effect."

For the first time in public, Cynthia's temper overran her control and vented itself on this convenient target. "I have never been so ill-used and insulted in my life!" she declared. "I do not forgive your aunt nor do I forgive you for sponsoring this jumped-up baggage! Good day, Mr. Cockerell!"

She swept off, further infuriated that her cousin made an apology to their host before following.

It was only when she had settled into her carriage and they were driving back to town that Cynthia realized what a scene she had created. Indeed, were she an unmarried young miss and not a widowed countess, she would be excluded from society for such goings-on.

As for Mr. Cockerell, the consequences remained to be seen. The worst of it, Lady Darnet reflected as she gritted her teeth and winced, was that his aunt had harped upon Cynthia's greatest weakness in front of him and Lady Jersey.

Well, she wasn't Margaret Linley, to flee to the country with her tail between her legs, she thought, lifting her chin. It wouldn't be long before Mr. Cockerell acknowledged that she was the lady he should marry.

Had Lady Darnet seen Edward at that moment, she would have felt less complacent. After staring at her retreating form with his hands clenched, he stalked across the garden to a secluded alcove where he could resolve his emotions safe from observation. Jumped-up baggage! That was what the wench had dared to call that sweet Angela Linley! Never had he imagined that Lady Darnet possessed such a viper's tongue. Always before, she had appeared the soul of good breeding.

The branches rustled nearby, and Mr. Cockerell turned to find himself facing the wide-eyed subject of his concern.

"Miss Linley." He knew he should declare her presence here unsuitable and escort her back to the others, but he could only stand and gaze at her.

The countess's remarks had brought a deep blush to her cheeks and a turquoise depth to her eyes, and Angela looked even more beautiful in the clear daylight than she had in the harsh shadows of Vauxhall. "Mr. Cockerell," she replied, "I'm truly sorry for what you've suffered."

"I?" he said. "Suffered?"

The girl clenched her hands in front of her. "This...
unpleasantness would never have occurred were it not for
your generosity toward us."

"It would never have occurred were it not for Lady Darnet's ill-nature," he corrected.

Surprise flashed across her face. "You blame her?"

"How could I not?" With difficulty, he refrained from
touching those bare shoulders and the milk-white skin of her
neck.

"I thought she...was someone special to you." Angela
lowered her gaze pensively. "Helen said you were courting
her. I thought I had given offence and forced your es-
trangement. I hadn't meant to cause you distress, Mr.
Cockerell."

"You didn't," he said. "It's true that I've called on her,
but I had never witnessed this aspect of her character before, and now..."

Edward paused to stare broodingly down at Angela.
Having so recently been enlightened as to the true spirit of
his former inamorata, he could not immediately trust any
woman. Was Angela's modesty mere pretence? Was she, like
Lady Darnet, a shrew in disguise?

"Perhaps we should go back," Angela suggested. "I
came after you without thinking, and I suppose it could be
considered improper."

Wordlessly he crooked his elbow and she placed her hand
upon it. Together, they strolled back into the midst of the
assembly.

Throughout the afternoon and evening, Edward continued to watch the girl. Her expressions fluctuated. Here she
smiled warmly; there she nodded politely; once or twice a
look of unhappiness flitted across her delicate face but was
quickly suppressed.

He wished he knew more of her. Now that she had become acceptable to society, no doubt the opportunity would present itself. Nevertheless, Edward determined silently, he would not go calling on the chit. He would never give his sister the satisfaction!

As for Angela, she was experiencing emotions for which her placid childhood had left her unprepared. Her feelings toward Mr. Cockerell had changed sharply from the previous week. At first, she had considered him harsh and rag-mannered. Then she had been forced to concede that at least he attempted to be fair, which was more than one could say of most members of the ton.

Today, seeing him again, she noticed a hundred small details that had escaped her before. His habit of rubbing the bridge of his nose when considering a serious matter; the way a smile transformed his sharp-featured face into gentleness; the erectness of his posture and the natural facility with which he assumed leadership of any situation.

Seeking him out privately had been foolhardy. But she hadn't been able to resist trying to learn whether he loved the countess, and her immense relief upon finding that he did not puzzled and frightened her.

Regarding him from across the lawn after their return, Angela was aware of a powerful desire to waltz close to him and inhale his rich masculine scent. Whatever could be the matter with her? she wondered. How could she have such feelings toward Edward Cockerell, whom even his own sister regarded as hard-hearted? He would never have given her a moment's consideration, had it not been for Helen's insistence!

So Angela passed the hours smiling and making conversation, never far from an awareness of her own tight-clenched heart. How she wished Meg were here to talk over the matter. Meg always had a common-sense solution to one's problems.

It cannot be that I love him! Angela thought in alarm. *If I do, then I must never let him know. He would only despise me.* Nor would she give him reason to think further ill of her, she decided, and went to seek out Helen.

The older girl greeted her merrily. "Are you having a good time?" she asked. "I heard about the contretemps with Lady Darnet, that witch! Thank goodness for Aunt Emily."

"Helen, I need your opinion on a serious matter." Angela drew her friend aside where no one would overhear.

"Yes?" Miss Cockerell raised an eyebrow.

"We haven't been entirely honest with your brother," Angela said. "As you know, I told him about Meg's eyesight, but I said nothing of our, er, financial situation." She watched her friend unhappily, aware that Helen had not been advised of the full truth, either.

"I know you've been on short rations for some time," the girl replied calmly. "Meg never said as much, but I could tell. And your dress. I'm sure no one else has recognized it, but I couldn't help doing so."

"Things are sorry indeed," Angela admitted. "Please don't let my mother know I told you! It's only that your brother will think he's been tricked if he learns the truth later. I believe we owe him our honesty."

"Oh, pooh!" said Helen. "He doesn't deserve it!"

"But he sponsored this garden party for me," Angela pointed out. "And because of me he quarrelled with Lady Darnet."

"Nevertheless," said the hostess with a sniff, "he has such a stiff-necked notion of honour that he might refuse to introduce you to eligible gentlemen unless they knew the whole truth."

"That's his right, if he wishes." Agitated, Angela twisted a fold of the silver gauze skirt in her hand.

"He might even refuse to let me frequent your company," Helen added ominously.

"I can't believe he would be so cruel as that!" cried Angela. "It's not our fault, and he is a fair-minded gentleman."

"Perhaps," said his sister. "But he would consider our patronage of you likely to entrap some other young man into an ill-considered marriage. Not that he could find you unsuitable, for you are well-bred. But you know that many families count upon the bride's marriage portion. For myself, I think love is all that matters, but Edward is impossible on the subject."

Impossible? Angela thought, gazing at Edward where he stood conversing with an elderly couple. She could only admire the fierceness of his convictions and the depth of his regard for honesty.

She still wished to tell him the truth about her situation, and would have done so had there been only her own welfare to consider. But she couldn't betray her mother and sister. Their futures must come first, even though protecting them might mean sacrificing the regard of the man Angela cherished.

"Well—" she linked arms with Helen "—let's not stand here gossiping like a pair of duchesses!"

Together the two girls moved forward to mingle with their guests.

CHAPTER TEN

EDWARD COCKERELL! Meg thought in amazement, reading Angela's letter for the third time. My sister in love with Edward Cockerell! The poor girl.

She laid aside the sheets of paper and stared out her bedroom window. For once, she failed to notice the crystal-clear details revealed even in twilight by her lorgnette.

If one were to believe Angela's letter, the gentleman had given no indication of returning the emotion. Indeed, it was difficult to imagine that particular fellow possessing any emotions whatsoever.

And she asks for my advice? Meg reflected woefully. *A fine one I am to be telling others how to handle their finer feelings!*

In the week since the party at Squire Roberts's, Meg had reached a painful conclusion of her own. She had fallen in love with Lord Bryn.

If Angela's chances of success were slim, her own were hopeless. The man was all but engaged to Miss Geraint, and furthermore showed no sign of developing a tendre for Meg. In fact, he had been scrupulously careful to keep a distance between them since that night.

Yet Meg looked for him everywhere, in spite of her best intentions. When she walked with the children in the garden, her heart leaped at the sight of his tall figure riding far-off on his stallion. When she conducted the lessons, she listened with one ear for the sound of his footsteps.

In vain, for the most part. The marquis had made a habit since last Saturday of calling upon the children only when they were in the care of the maid Jenny.

Meg had even begun giving Vanessa deportment lessons as an excuse for marching her up and down the front stairs. No doubt the sound of girlish laughter had given his lordship sufficient warning, and he had kept away.

I? Give advice?

With a mirthless laugh, Meg turned from the window and drew out her pen and paper. The time had come to tell her mother and sister the truth.

Perhaps not the entire truth; no need to confess the futile attachment she had formed. But they must know where she was, and under what pretence.

Her mother could best advise her whether to continue on to Derby or return to London. For in another week Miss Geraint and her family would be arriving, and Meg was determined to leave then.

She tried to imagine her family's reactions. Amusement and admiration, perhaps, on Angela's part; shock and outrage, justifiably, on Lady Mary's.

Guiltily Meg wondered if she had betrayed her mother's trust in her. A harmless misunderstanding—but why had she played along with it these past two weeks?

The answer, she had to admit, was that her affection for Lord Bryn had begun the moment she'd first set eyes on him, however blurrily, as he rode up with those two ragamuffins in tow. His easy manner, both with the children and with the woman he thought to be their governess, had contrasted delightfully with the pompous gentlemen she had known in town.

Not only that, but she had come to understand from the moment he kissed her, what it meant to be a woman. Such mysteries were kept carefully from the ears of unmarried misses. The marriage bed, so far as Meg had known, was a place for sleeping and, by some unknown means, for conceiving children.

Even now, she had only vague suspicions of its true purpose, but they were solidifying night by night. Dreams troubled her slumber, dreams in which the marquis drew her close against his body, making her flesh burn with indescribable sensations. She longed to return his wild kisses, to feel his touch upon her soft skin...

Was this love? Or only wantonness against which to shield oneself even in marriage? Would a husband be shocked by such abandon? Meg wished desperately that she knew.

Wrenching her thoughts back to the task at hand, she began to compose a letter to her mother and sister.

THE ANSWERS CAME BACK swiftly. Meg read Lady Mary's first. Her mother expressed dismay, but also understanding. She, too, had been young once, and knew that Meg's high spirits had been much confined by her dismal experiences in London and her inability to see properly.

If no one were the wiser, Meg might perhaps escape censure. Neither Lord Bryn nor Germaine Geraint ever came to town; and should Germaine's cousins learn the truth, neither Helen nor Edward were likely to talk. Helen might be a gossip, but her loyalty to Meg was such that she would not risk hurting her.

"Lord Bryn is reputed for his proper conduct, and so I know that nothing untoward has occurred, but one must be concerned with appearances," Lady Mary wrote. "It is imperative that you leave as soon as possible."

Then came the part that softened Meg's pain. "Matters are well in hand here in town, and Mr. Brummell has made it clear he harbours no resentment against you.

"Since you inform me that Lord Bryn has paid you generous wages, you may use them, if you wish, to take the mail coach back to London. I cannot promise that you will find many of your dresses remaining unaltered, but at least we may enjoy your company. We miss you very much.''

Angela's letter was livelier but at the same time sadder. She wrote that they were invited everywhere, even to Almack's, and had been out nearly every night. Mr. Cockerell and Helen often joined them, but although he spent considerable time in Angela's company, Edward showed no sign of affection.

"My only consolation lies in the fact that he displays no warmth toward Lady Darnet when we encounter her,'' Angela went on. "What do you suppose this signifies? Is he attempting to make her jealous by attending on me, or does he do it only at Helen's insistence?''

Meg wished she knew the answer.

Well, she had her own plans to make. The Geraints would be arriving Friday next. Meg decided that to prevent undue disruption to the children, she could remain until Monday, but no longer. Then it would be the task of their future mother to supervise the hiring of a new governess.

She requested an audience with his lordship and was told he would see her in his study. Carefully she reviewed in her mind the tale she'd composed, having decided that after their embrace the truth would only embarrass them both unduly.

Never having visited this masculine room before, Meg entered timidly. Such a dark chamber, she thought, observing the mahogany furniture and deep-stained leather. How the marquis suited it, standing behind his desk, an ominous frown on his countenance.

"How may I help you, Miss Linley?'' he asked

Meg clutched her hands together nervously. "My lord, I've received a letter from my mother. She writes that she is ill and begs me to return to London.''

His eyes flew to hers, and they contained an expression Meg couldn't read. "I'm sorry to hear that. I hope she will be soon mended."

"She didn't say." Meg inhaled deeply. "I realize this comes at an inconvenient time, with your visitors on their way. I thought I might remain until Monday."

"The children will miss you deeply." His lordship tapped one finger upon the desk top. "Are you certain this is so great a crisis as to require your permanent departure? Perhaps a visit of a week or two—"

"I think not," Meg said. "I was given to understand she will need a nurse for some time."

There was nothing more to be said between them, and no words to say it. The air crackled with unspoken longings—at least for Meg.

"Very well," said the marquis at last. "I will have arrangements made for your conveyance."

"Thank you, my lord." Meg curtseyed and turned away.

"Miss Linley?"

"Yes?" She looked back.

"You may keep the lorgnette," he said. "We wouldn't want you getting on the wrong carriage."

Meg nodded dumbly and hurried away. He had meant the remark as a jest, of course, a reference to the "joke" she had told when she arrived; but for some reason she found herself near tears.

Later, in the schoolroom, Tom took the news with difficulty, his small face crumpling and sobs wracking his frame. Meg held him close.

Vanessa took a more pragmatic viewpoint. "When I have my come-out, will you be in town to advise me how to go on?" she asked.

"I certainly hope so." Meg felt grateful for the distraction, since she feared the girl might join Tom in his weeping. "Although that's a few years away."

The girl shrugged off this minor inconvenience. "Nevertheless, you shall assist me. I would like that very much. I shall have lots of new gowns, and you can tell me the best dressmakers."

"Oh, don't be such a prattle-box!" wailed Tom. "Why can't Uncle Andrew marry you, Miss Linley, instead of that . . . that Miss Geraint!"

"Don't you like her?" Meg asked.

"We've never met her." Vanessa wrinkled her nose. "But I'm sure I shan't like her at all. She never goes to London and they say her wardrobe is abominable." Her tongue twisted a bit over that last word, but she managed to make herself understood.

"I'm sure you'll love her," Meg said briskly. "And since you'll have no one to give you lessons next week, we shall work doubly hard today. Ready?"

They nodded reluctantly, and the business of daily living gradually took the edge off Tom's misery.

On Thursday morning, the day before the Geraints were to arrive, Lord Bryn gave Meg permission to ride with Mrs. Franklin into the town of Macclesfield. Although farther afield than Stockport and Marple, it boasted some excellent shops.

Jenny was away, helping her ailing sister, and so the children were entrusted to the timorous Bertha.

"She'll do well enough. They never drop the mouse down anyone's skirts twice," said Mrs. Franklin as she and Meg set off in the curricle.

Once in town, Meg selected hair ribbons for herself and gifts to take Lady Mary and Angela. For her mother, she chose a pair of gloves, and for her sister a lace-edged handkerchief which could be used to fill in a low neckline when the season ended and they retreated to the country.

Mrs. Franklin took considerably longer selecting household items. Meg spent the time strolling about the silk-manufacturing town, admiring its medieval architecture, hilly streets, and the picturesque black-and-white-timbered houses she had come to love.

The two women treated themselves to luncheon at the Cat and Fiddle Inn in a splendid moorland setting three miles to the east.

"It's right sorry I am that you'll be leaving," said Mrs. Franklin. "By the by, Lord Bryn mentioned that you're invited to attend the ball he's holding for the Geraints Saturday night."

Meg bit her lip. Suppose someone there should know her? Unlikely, but dangerous. However, she saw no polite way to decline. And after all, the only ones at the ball would be the Geraint family and the neighbours.

"I fear I haven't a proper gown," she said.

Mrs. Franklin waved away the objection. "With your beauty, girl, you'd look splendid in my old gingham! And your clothes may not be fancy, but they're quality."

The real objection, Meg admitted to herself as they returned home in the curricle, was that at the ball the marquis was expected to announce his engagement. Would she be able to hide her unhappiness and congratulate the couple as she ought?

You got yourself into this situation, Meg Linley, and you shall carry it off! she commanded in a mental approximation of Lady Mary's tones.

They arrived at Brynwood to find the place in turmoil.

"The bloody children have disappeared again!" snapped the marquis, his temper overcoming his usual good manners. "They're nowhere to be found, and Bertha's in hysterics, shrieking about a ghost."

Meg fought back a smile. "Have you searched the attic? Vanessa tells me they like to play dress-up."

"We've looked in all the usual places," Mr. Franklin interjected smoothly. "We believe they may have gone berrying again, as they did the day you arrived, Miss Linley."

"Then I shall go and look for them." Unwilling in her haste to take the time to change her clothes—her attire was sensible enough—Meg set off in southerly direction. Lord Bryn and the servants headed off elsewhere.

It was well past midday, Meg noted as she started out. She wasn't yet overly concerned for the children's safety, but she knew that Tom would do whatever Vanessa said, and it was impossible to tell what notion the girl might have taken into her head.

After a time, Meg's voice grew hoarse with calling and her legs began to ache with the unaccustomed walking. Still she pushed on, growing more and more anxious as the sun descended through the western sky.

At last she saw a figure on the horizon, north of her. A man and horse.

He galloped toward her, and Meg saw that it was Lord Bryn. At any other time, she would have been lost in admiration of his fine figure and splendid horsemanship, but now she waited in a torment of anxiety for news of the runaways.

When the rider drew up, Meg saw with relief that he was smiling. "We've found the little rascals!" he called. "They were in your room, Miss Linley, playing dress-up with your clothes!"

Meg smiled ruefully. "If only I'd gone up to change before coming out to look!"

"You must be weary." His lordship swung down from King Arthur. "I'll give you a ride back, then."

She regarded him dubiously. "I'm hardly attired for riding, Lord Bryn." Indeed, Meg had never ridden astride, for Lady Mary insisted that a gentlewoman rode only sidesaddle.

"There's no one to notice or care," he replied. Relief at finding the children had dispelled his dour mood, and he grinned boyishly.

"Oh?" Meg gazed up at the horse, which looked enormous. "Are you sure this isn't an elephant, my lord? He seems large enough to me."

"What? My Meg a coward?" he challenged. Without giving her time to reflect on his use of her given name and the possessive pronoun, Bryn clamped his hands about her waist to lift her.

The warmth of his touch sent a delicate shiver down her spine. Attempting to dispel it, Meg reached for a grip on the saddle, but she lost her balance and fell back down against the marquis. He caught her easily, his arms encircling her, his cheek pressed against her hair. They both stood motionless, overcome by this unexpected contact.

Meg's skin tingled, her knees felt wobbly, and her entire body seemed to suffuse with warmth as the marquis turned her gently round to face him. His hands moved to her shoulders, then framed her face as his mouth descended slowly to hers.

Meg had no desire to protest as her lips parted. Instead, she clung to him, letting hunger well within her as the kiss deepened.

This, this was the stuff of her dreams, this raging in the blood. It was more than she had imagined, the feeling of his body against hers, the excitement rising in her as she drank in his caresses. They could not seem to stop kissing, pressing close, their heat merging and intensifying until it seemed they would burst into flames.

It was Lord Bryn who drew away finally. "My Meg," he whispered. "What's happening to us?"

"I don't know." What a tangle! How she wished she'd never deceived this man. But had she not, Meg knew, she'd never have discovered such passion. How could she live without him now?

"Must you leave?" he murmured, trailing small kisses across her brow, nose, and cheeks.

"My lord, I..." Meg swallowed, trying to clear a path for the words. "There are matters I should make clear. My arrival here, my station. You see..."

"You're overwrought, dearest." He stepped back, still holding her hands. "Tonight, after dinner, you and I must talk privately."

She nodded dumbly. Yes, tonight. How angry he would be when he learned the truth! Would that coldness, which she had seen before, envelop him? Would he send her away? Her thoughts awhirl, Meg let herself be lifted onto King Arthur and felt the horse shift as the marquis swung up in front of her.

Arms clasped around Lord Bryn, her body arched against his back, Meg closed her eyes as they rode forward. She could feel every motion of the stallion ripple through the man. The three of them became one, riding through the dusk. *I love him,* Meg thought. *I want to stay with him forever. Please let this dream never end.*

The gallop muted into a canter and she knew they were nearing Brynwood. With a sigh, Meg pushed a wayward strand of hair out of her eyes.

She hoped no one was looking out of the house as the canter slowed to a trot. For she could imagine the picture she made, riding astride with her arms around the marquis and her hair floating loose.

They rounded the corner of the house and came to an abrupt halt. Almost dislodged from her seat, Meg clutched the marquis for balance before straightening. She removed the lorgnette from its safe haven in her pocket and leaned out to gaze around him.

A large tan-and-umber carriage stood in the drive. Vaguely, in the background, Meg noted the Franklins mingling with several servants in unfamiliar livery. Her eyes quickly riveted on the figures in front, an older couple and a younger, stern-faced woman, staring at the two of them with undisguised astonishment.

The Geraints had arrived early.

CHAPTER ELEVEN

IN THE DAYS FOLLOWING the garden party, Edward Cockerell became a stranger to himself. In outward appearances, he was much the same. He arose early, breakfasted alone, and went to the City to conduct business and talk with his man of affairs. Or, if that wasn't necessary, he remained in his study reviewing the rents and other matters of the family's estates.

Yet his thoughts betrayed him. Deucedly annoying, how he fussed now with the cravat which had never troubled him before; how he vexed his valet by rejecting first one waistcoat and then another; how when driving he found himself watching for someone or something he couldn't identify.

It was time to put his life back in order.

Having received an apologetic note from Lady Darnet explaining that she had suffered from a toothache, he visited her to see if matters between them might be patched up. She received him in her gold parlour, with an elderly female cousin dozing in one corner for propriety's sake. Gowned in dark blue satin, the countess reigned as an Incomparable.

Why, then, could Edward not forget how harsh her skin had looked in the daylight and the hardness about her eyes? The toothache was the explanation, she had said, and for her display of temper, as well. It should have eased his doubts, but it did not.

He noted for the first time the absence of warmth between him and the countess, the lack of any spark when their eyes chanced to meet, the way she confined her conversation to malicious on-dits. Oddly, Edward felt as if he were comparing her to someone. It was not until he was returning home in his phaeton that he realized who that someone was.

Angela Linley.

She was the figure who haunted the corners of his mind. She was the ghost who shadowed his dreams.

The discovery rocked through him like cannon-fire. Angela Linley? That young girl, his sister's barely acceptable friend? It could not be, must not be. The chit was entirely too lively and unrestrained to meet his standards for matrimony.

He was, after all, heir to considerable monies and served as trustee for not only his sister but also his aunt and two young cousins. There were tenants to consider, and dozens of servants, including some who had waited upon his parents and grandparents. If Edward lost his good sense and allied himself with an unpredictable, overemotional wife, great harm might come of it.

He recalled only too well the plight of a schoolmate of his at Eton, Jamie Winter. When Jamie's mother lost her temper and insulted Queen Charlotte, he had been removed from school and his sister's engagement to the eldest son of a duke had been promptly terminated. After the family was forced to retreat to the country, the daughter had died of a fever—some said she committed suicide—and Jamie had departed for America, never to be heard from again.

Such, Edward reflected grimly, might be the fate of his own offspring if he married Angela. Nevertheless, the girl did come from good family. For the first time in his life, he found himself unsure of the proper course.

The answer came to him slowly, as he mulled over the matter during the next few hours. If Angela was a ghost, then she could be exorcised. Not through priestly ministrations, but through the dulling effect of habituation.

He refused to allow himself to visit her alone, which might cause society to think he was courting. It would be improper, of course, to woo and then abandon a respectable young woman. Therefore, on the following day, Edward decided to call on the Linleys in the company of Helen, sitting silently while the two girls conversed in animated fashion.

How lovely Angela looked, he couldn't help but notice. Sternly, he forced himself to concentrate upon her flaws.

Her conversation was unsuitable. Interesting, true, and never unkind, but entirely too well informed. What well-bred young lady of the ton would keep so abreast of the war with France, and so forcefully decry it for raising the price of food and thereby increasing hunger among the English poor?

Admirable sentiments in a man, he thought, or perhaps in an older woman, but inappropriate in a young girl. Angela even dared to criticize the enclosure laws that forced small farmers off the land. Politics was no matter for a female, particularly not when one of her visitors was a large landowner whose estates benefitted from the enclosures. She might even, he reflected with horror, have the temerity to broach such unpopular opinions in the company of other lords and ladies. If so, she would surely be shunned.

Yet as the days went by and Edward adhered to his plan by visiting repeatedly with Helen, he was forced to concede that the family behaved in a manner beyond reproach. The Linleys avoided the excesses in which many other families with a marriageable daughter indulged. There was no flaunting of jewels and gowns, nor a plethora of sumptuous balls, merely the good taste and refinement one found among the old nobility. Yes, Angela Linley would make a splendid wife for some less-particular gentleman, but not, he warned himself, for Edward Cockerell.

So matters might have remained had it not been for Sir Manfred and Lady Darnet.

When Edward failed to pay a second call upon the countess, she decided it was time to take matters into her own hands. Cynthia had no inkling that Edward already considered Angela unsuitable, but she well knew the young man's extreme adherence to propriety. To place Angela Linley in an unflattering public light would quickly destroy his interest in her, the countess believed.

To this end she required the assistance of her cousin, the baronet. Cynthia invited him to tea and told him of jests, which she herself invented, which Angela had made at his expense at a card party. These bon mots, the countess declared, were currently circulating through the ton. With shrewd insight, Cynthia abused her cousin's vanity in a way calculated to provoke him most painfully.

Sir Manfred was easily persuaded that the Linley minx had played him for a fool. Within the hour, he had become Angela's most bitter enemy.

Smoothly Cynthia proposed a plan. Sir Manfred would pretend to court the Linley girl and be seen with her everywhere. Then he would contrive, with Lady Darnet's help if need be, to create an embarrassing situation in which she would appear to be at fault. During this courtship, the countess proposed that she spread titbits about Angela. Nothing so scandalous as to defy belief, but needle pricks which would help lay the groundwork for the upstart's ultimate downfall.

By the time her cousin left her parlour, Cynthia's irritation with Angela Linley had muted into glee. That frothy little baggage would rue the day she ever set her cap for Edward Cockerell!

The conspiracy took its first step at the Opera, where London society had gone ostensibly to watch the melodrama of *Timour the Tartar* and a pantomime with the clown Joey Grimaldi. In truth, everyone had come to be seen and to show off the latest fashions and hairstyles, with little regard for what was transpiring on stage.

It was Angela's first visit to Covent Garden, and she descended eagerly amid the crush of carriages. She paused to stare up at the massive building which had opened less than two years earlier to replace a structure destroyed by fire. The ponderous exterior of stucco and stone, relieved only by a Greek portico resting on four Doric columns, struck Angela as unexpectedly severe, but the interior more than made up for it.

The Linleys and the Cockerells, who had come together, entered at Bow Street. There they proceeded through the foyer and up the main staircase, a single grand flight set off dramatically by a vault resting on black Ionic columns.

At the top, they entered a curving lobby, from which branched a long saloon styled in the Greek manner and lined with statues. Here Edward purchased refreshments before escorting the party to the Cockerells' private box.

Painted a Grecian pink accented by mahogany woodwork, it was set forward in one of the horseshoe tiers of boxes. These overlooked the pit, where poorer folk and rowdy young bucks sat. Raucous catcalls and the smells of unwashed bodies ascended forcefully, but were ignored by the elegant set, who conversed in a more seemly fashion.

Angela's gaze travelled upward to the curving, ornamental ceiling, before Lady Mary distracted her by pointing out some of their acquaintances in other boxes. Nods, smiles, and waves were exchanged. How exciting this was! At last she was part of the glittering world of which she had dreamed for so long.

The entertainment began, but no one paid much attention. Even Angela, in her excitement, found it difficult to focus on the absurd goings-on of the melodrama.

She had little inkling that a different sort of drama was about to unfold.

At the interval, the real business of the evening began. Gentlemen and ladies visited back and forth between boxes, exchanging compliments and gossip.

Lady Darnet was a popular figure as always, and she glowed with delight, the reason for which, as she alone knew, derived from having observed that Angela Linley's gown bore a strong resemblance to one the girl's sister had worn the previous season.

"Do you know," the countess murmured to Lady Jersey, "that the Linley creature is wearing one of her sister's made-over dresses? The family must have fallen upon hard times, or they are extremely clutch-fisted."

Cynthia had intended, by singling out the leader of society, to spread her tale directly to the top. What she failed to take into account, however, was that Lady Jersey was no fool. The patroness knew perfectly well what lay behind Lady Darnet's remarks.

Therefore it was to Edward Cockerell, as Angela's sponsor, that Lady Jersey took this item. His response was an immediate denial, followed for emphasis by the statement that he believed his sister had accompanied Miss Angela to the dressmaker.

Now why had he said that? Edward wondered after Lady Jersey departed. No matter; it would put the preposterous story to rest.

He had not meant to leap so strongly to Angela's defence. Might not his championing of her lead to speculation? Yet he was infuriated that anyone should subject the Linleys to idle gossip and speculation. He might not choose

Angela for himself, but he accorded her a certain grudging respect.

Meanwhile, Sir Manfred was laying the groundwork for his counterfeit suit. Ensconced in the Cockerell box with the three ladies he found there, he proceeded to ply Angela with witticisms which soon had her laughing.

"You are indeed clever, Sir Manfred!" she declared.

Her apparently genuine admiration flattered his sensibilities, until he remembered the cruelties which his cousin had said she had uttered behind his back. The baronet harrumphed mightily. "How kind you are. And how very lovely this evening. May I compliment you on that particularly becoming gown? And you, as well, Miss Cockerell. A bevy of beauties. Well. Such splendid company. I cannot tear myself away...."

His back was to the entrance and so he failed to see the dark look which crossed Edward's face when he entered and spied them sitting together. Sir Manfred had intended to remain in place for the second act, but he found himself firmly steered away by Mr. Cockerell and thrust from the box with a firmness approaching insult.

"Can't understand it," muttered the baronet as he rejoined Lady Darnet. "Fellow was practically rude to me!"

Cynthia shook her head, lost in her own conjectures. Why had Lady Jersey not spread the gossip? For if she had, word of it would surely have reached herself by now. And how far had matters got, if Edward still behaved in such a proprietary manner toward Angela?

The countess was not dissuaded, however. Despite the failure of her first attempt, she resolved to continue passing along such titbits in the future. One of them would surely strike to the heart.

In the following days, Sir Manfred frequently visited the Linley household, ignoring the coldness displayed him by Mr. Cockerell when they chanced to meet. He took Angela driving in Hyde Park, plied her with flowers, and generally gave everyone to believe he was dangling after her.

The girl had other suitors, but none so persistent. Most were fops still tied to their parents' purse strings, or younger sons who must marry an heiress, which she was not believed to be.

As the days passed, the baronet found himself enjoying more and more the sweetness of Angela's disposition. When he dropped the reins during a ride through the park, she made a game of it, and soon had them both laughing. He was even given to understand by an acquaintance that she had chastised an acquaintance who poked fun at the baronet's girth.

Sir Manfred began to wonder at the cutting remarks his cousin had attributed to this delightful miss. Had she truly made them? Didn't suit her character. Must have been misheard. How like Cynthia to put the worst interpretation on things. Impossible to remain angry with such a taking little thing.

Indeed, the baronet was having thoughts of entirely another nature. He'd never been eager to find himself leg-shackled, but if a man must marry, he could scarcely do better than Angela Linley.

Lady Darnet's noose was developing snarls, although she did not yet know of them. Another such concerned the reactions of her intended husband, Edward Cockerell.

Often, when he and Helen came to call on the Linleys they found Sir Manfred there before them, and he stayed until they left. At other times Angela was away from home, having gone driving with that same gentleman.

Sir Manfred! Driving home from the Linleys' on such an occasion, Edward clenched his fists and would have pounded the seat but for his sister's presence. He had nearly succeeded in dissuading himself from further involvement with the young lady, but the presumption of the baronet infuriated him.

"I think it entirely too unfortunate," said Helen.

"What?" Her brother glared at her, resenting the interruption of his thoughts.

"That Angela should marry such a...weak sort of chap," she said with a sniff.

"Marry?" Edward wished his heart wouldn't pound in that annoying manner.

"Well, I don't suppose he's asked her yet, but clearly he will," Helen went on. "I don't think he's right for her."

"Then she must refuse him." Edward felt his pulse return to normal and his common sense reassert itself.

"How can she?" said Helen. "He's her only serious suitor. And she's seen only too well the pitfalls into which a girl can fall if she goes unmarried for long. She'd hardly dare wait and risk some other scandal, especially with a certain person spreading false rumours about her."

"I beg your pardon?" Edward said.

"Far be it from me to name any names," Helen replied. "But I have contradicted two nasty stories this week, and I can only guess where they started."

With a shock, Edward remembered Lady Jersey and the nonsense about Angela's gown. Had she told him where she heard it? Oh, yes, it had been repeated to her by Lady Darnet.

Repeated. Or invented?

This revelation so disturbed the young man that he steered his horses perilously near an apple cart and nearly overturned the phaeton.

"Edward!" cried his sister. "Do you want to kill us both?"

He clamped his mouth shut grimly and drove the rest of the way home without speaking.

The correct course of action became clear to Edward that night. He had balanced the many factors: Miss Angela's merits against her demerits, his own responsibility as her sponsor, and his sister's affection for her.

The logical solution was that he himself should marry the girl. With a firm hand, she would shape up to be an excellent wife. He would coach her on what subjects to avoid in conversation and on how to restrain her natural enthusiasms. She was young, and therefore biddable. It was a wise and dispassionate decision, and Edward congratulated himself.

In view of the rival courtship of Sir Manfred, it also struck Edward as perfectly natural that he should drive to the Linleys' house the next morning at ten o'clock, so early that Angela was still at breakfast when he arrived.

He asked to speak to Lady Mary alone. When she came, he told her briefly of his intentions. If she was surprised, she gave no sign of it, saying merely, "You have my permission, if my daughter wishes to marry you."

Lady Mary returned to the breakfast room and sent Angela to see him.

"Mr. Cockerell!" She had dashed to the parlour, but now hesitated on the threshold. "Perhaps we could walk in the garden?"

He agreed at once. This suited his purpose, and furthermore he was pleased that she refrained from joining him in a private room unchaperoned, which would have been improper under ordinary circumstances. Of course she didn't yet know why he had come.

As they strolled through the garden, Angela kept her face averted and pointed out the various flowers.

Edward cleared his throat. "You may wonder what brings me here at this hour of the morning, and without my sister."

"Oh, you are always welcome, Mr. Cockerell," she said politely.

"Thank you." He gestured to a stone bench and she obediently sat upon it.

The next motion required of him affronted Edward's dignity, and he hesitated. To get down upon one's knees, on a walkway composed of small sharp stones! It was enough to ruin one's temper, not to mention one's trousers.

Nevertheless, it was customary, and Edward had no intention of flouting tradition. He adjusted his dark blue pantaloons and lowered himself onto the pathway. "Miss Angela, will you do me the honour of becoming my wife?"

She stared at him in astonishment. "Do you mean...? That was why my mother... But you never even hinted... Can you really mean it, Edward?"

This curious speech might have given him pause but for the pleasure of hearing his given name upon her lips. Considering his duty performed, Edward removed himself from his uncomfortable position, dusted off his trousers, and sat on the bench. "You may indeed consider my proposal surprising, in view of our different temperaments," he said.

"Well, yes, I suppose so," the girl murmured. There was a warm radiance to her face and she leaned ever so slightly toward him.

Edward's arguments came back to him now. "We must consider the purpose of matrimony," he explained. "It is, naturally, to produce heirs."

"It is?" said Angela.

"Indeed, and of course to maintain one's position in society," he continued. "We are eminently well suited. Your bloodlines are impeccable, you have been a success in society, you are young and pure, our families have become close friends, and I am nearly thirty and have an obligation to settle down."

"I see." Inexplicably, the girl looked crestfallen. "What about the finer emotions, Mr. Cockerell?"

"Love?" he said. "An overrated sensation, I should think. Oh, it's well enough for poets to write about, but it hasn't much place in everyday life. Can you imagine what a state the world would be in, if everyone married for love?"

"In this we disagree, then." Angela looked thoughtful.

"You need not tender your answer immediately," Edward said, wishing he could read her thoughts. But what possible objection could she have? "I do hope you won't keep me waiting long."

The girl took a deep breath. "I shan't keep you waiting at all. The answer is yes, Mr. Cockerell. I should be pleased to marry you."

The exultation which shot through Edward was entirely inappropriate, and he subdued it ruthlessly. "I believe you have made a wise decision," he remarked, before rising and escorting Angela back to her parent.

Well done, old chap, he told himself on the drive home. *That should pluck Sir Manfred's goose!*

"YOU NEEDN'T MARRY HIM if you will be unhappy," Lady Mary was telling her daughter in the parlour at that very moment. "Although it is an excellent match."

"Oh, Mother, I love him!" Angela cried. "If only he felt that way about me!"

"Why are you so certain he does not?" the elder woman asked as she mended a torn blouse.

"He prattled on and on about duty and heirs and breeding." Angela jumped up and paced restlessly. "As if I were some sort of cattle!"

"Perhaps that is merely his way," suggested Lady Mary. "Gentlemen aren't as expressive as we ladies, you know."

"Expressive?" Angela shook her head. "Stiff as a log! I must be out of my head to love him, but I do and I plan to marry him even if he doesn't care a fig for me."

"Well spoken," said her mother.

Angela picked up her embroidery and sat pondering the matter a while longer before asking, "Mother, did he discuss my dowry?"

"Why, no," said Lady Mary. "Of course that is untouched. I would have sold my jewels before I used that money."

"I know that." Her daughter jabbed a needle into her embroidery. "But it's so unlike Edward Cockerell not to discuss something of that nature."

"Never mind," said her mother. "Meg will be coming home on Tuesday."

Angela uttered a silent prayer. *Please don't let Edward find out that my sister has been masquerading as a governess. If he does, he'll surely throw me over or require that I renounce her.*

She would, of course, stick by Meg no matter what. Angela fervently hoped the problem would not arise.

CHAPTER TWELVE

BEFORE THE AWKWARD MOMENT could lengthen unbearably, Lord Bryn dismounted. Leaving one of the grooms to aid Meg, he strode toward his visitors.

"Mr. and Mrs. Geraint, Miss Geraint," he acknowledged. "Forgive this strange appearance, but my niece and nephew disappeared for a time. Their governess was out seeking them and so, after they were found safe, I rode out to fetch her."

Mrs. Geraint, a wispy, pale sort of woman, sniffed. "A carriage would have been more proper."

"Oh, piffle, Mother!" declared her daughter, who looked entirely too large to have emerged from such a small parent. Tall and rawboned, Miss Geraint closely resembled her father in appearance but not in speech, for he remained silent while she discoursed freely. "One can hardly be expected to drive a carriage where there is no road!"

"Well, she might have stayed upon the road, then," Mrs. Geraint said stubbornly.

"Stuff and nonsense!" bellowed Germaine. "The object was to find the children, not to take a carriage ride with Lord Bryn!"

She strode over to where Meg stood brushing off her skirts. "Hope he didn't give you too bruising a ride, miss. Or perhaps you're a horsewoman?"

"I'm afraid not." Meg smiled apologetically, unable to resist liking this forthright person. She tapped her lorgnette. "My vision is too poor."

"Ah. Quite right." The tall woman nodded and then, in a manner which would have astounded the assembly at Almack's, seized Meg's hand and pumped it as if they were men. "Glad to meet you. My name's Germaine Geraint. Funny sort of name, ain't it? Sounds like a Frenchie."

Meg laughed. "I'm Meg Linley, and I'm delighted to meet you. Now if you'll excuse me, I think I should change my clothes."

"Indeed you should." To everyone's amazement, Germaine linked her arm through Meg's and strolled inside with her, as if it were the most normal thing in the world for the future lady of the manor to befriend the children's governess.

What did one say to such an Original? Meg couldn't think of anything clever, so she inquired politely, "Did you have a nice journey?"

"Oh, well enough, well enough," boomed Germaine as they ascended the stairs. Rustling noises informed Meg that the servants were peering out from every crack and cranny. "As nice as one can have when Mother's in one of her moods."

"I beg your pardon?" Meg wasn't certain a lowly governess should encourage such talk.

"As you heard," the woman replied, "she wants everything in its place, and if there is no place, she would shove it into one which doesn't suit. Why, only this morning she took umbrage at seeing a bird flying north. ''Tis the wrong season,' she told me. 'That bird has no propriety.'"

Meg could well imagine those words issuing from Mrs. Geraint's dry lips, and chuckled as they reached the bedrooms.

Meg's chamber was in the guest wing, a singular honour since most of the servants slept in the attic. "Surely you would like to supervise your unpacking and freshen up," Meg said as they paused on the threshold of her room.

"Not at all," declared Miss Geraint. "Been cooped up in a carriage with my parents for the better part of two days, and that's more than one can properly bear. I need to be out and about."

Meg felt awkward, changing her clothes in front of a veritable stranger, but the other woman's friendly chatter soon put her at ease. "Difficult children, are they?" Germaine asked as Meg splashed herself with water from the ewer. "Good thing we've got you with us, then."

Meg seized the moment to inform Miss Geraint of her forthcoming departure to aid her mother. The woman clucked sympathetically. "Ill, is she? We've got an old woman in our village, who can cure most anything, or so people say. Wouldn't know myself—I've never been sick."

Meg could well imagine.

As soon as the governess was restored, Germaine insisted on going up to visit the children. "Little spitfires, eh?" she asked as they mounted toward the nursery. "Chip off the old block, I'd say."

"They're really very dear," Meg admitted. "I've grown quite attached to them during my few weeks here."

"What? You've only just come? What a pity you must leave so soon!" Germaine spoke almost entirely in exclamations. "A few weeks—that's hardly a proper visit, let alone employment. Are you certain you can't bring your mother here?"

Such a possibility had never been broached before, and Meg was caught off guard. "There's my younger sister, also—"

"Oh, bring her, too, by all means." Fortunately Germaine was distracted at this point when they entered the nursery and witnessed two rebellious small faces peering out from their beds.

"Put to sleep early, are you?" said Miss Geraint. "Given everyone a difficult day, and you deserve it."

"We didn't do anything bad," said Vanessa, pouting. "We were only playing dress-up with Miss Linley's clothes."

"And frightened Bertha half to death by pretending to be ghosts," Meg scolded.

"Ghosts?" Germaine stared at the children with admiration. "That's a new one. When I was a child I got rid of nurses by putting a mouse down their skirts."

"Terror lives over there." Meg pointed at the box and, comprehension dawning, Germaine reached in and lifted out the squeaking rodent.

"Oh, he's a lively devil," she declared, holding the mouse in one hand and stroking his back with a finger. "This Bertha sounds like a weak dish of tea."

"She is!" Tom bounced up and down on his bed. "We were left with her all day. I think it was wrong of Miss Linley to go into town with Mrs. Franklin when she's going to be leaving us so soon."

"The world doesn't revolve around you, young man." Germaine fixed him with a stern eye.

"Are you going to be our mother?" asked Vanessa. "I don't like your clothes."

Meg suppressed an urge to rebuke the child. In fact, Miss Geraint's gown was a skillfully cut fine grey muslin, though it hung awkwardly on her large-boned frame.

"Clothes ain't all that important," the future Lady Bryn replied amiably. "You've a lot to learn about life, young miss. Were you put to bed without supper?"

"Yes!" cried Vanessa.

"No," Tom corrected in a small voice. "Jenny gave us bread and milk."

"More than you deserve!" Chuckling, Germaine swept out of the room with the governess in her wake. *She likes them, and they're going to adore her,* Meg thought, wishing she didn't feel this pang of envy.

To the servants' astonishment, Miss Geraint insisted that Meg join them at dinner that night. "I've taken a liking to her," she said.

"As you wish," Lord Bryn acquiesced. His eyes swept past Meg without appearing to see her, and she felt as though she'd become invisible.

Would they ever have that conversation they'd planned? She wished she knew what he had intended to say, and how he would have responded to the truth about herself. Perhaps it was just as well that they part on neutral terms.

Or was it, Meg wondered as they sat down to simple country fare of roast mutton and duck, green beans and salad. She loved him so much that her heart felt near cracking at the prospect of her departure.

She could not imagine ever responding to another man this way, her skin tingling in his presence, her soul filling with strange yearnings, her lips longing to touch his. If it was true that there was only one man created for her in the universe, then this must be he.

But it was too late now. His intended—albeit no engagement had yet been formally announced—was here with them, and Meg liked her very much. Further, she could see that with such an unorthodox temperament, Germaine might never find another husband. It would be the height of villainy to supplant her.

At dinner, Miss Geraint kept them royally entertained. With her colourful way of speaking, she could hold an audience transfixed describing a rabbit which nearly dashed out its life under the wheels of their carriage, or telling of a fox hunt in which two horses barely avoided tumbling down one atop the other through the clumsiness of their riders.

Meg wished she had known her under other circumstances so that they might have become friends. She sneaked a glance at Lord Bryn. Surely he must admire her, as well.

He wore a pleasant expression and attended Miss Geraint with interest. Yet, in spite of herself, Meg was relieved to see no sign of anything more than a mild affection.

She knew so little of marriage. Perhaps those quiverings in her body when Lord Bryn embraced her had been the sensations of a lost soul, a secret wanton. Perhaps such response was unsuitable in a wife.

After dinner, when the women retired to the drawing room, Meg excused herself and went upstairs. She would have enjoyed more of Germaine's company, but Mrs. Geraint looked fiercely put out at having to hobnob with a mere servant.

Meg's mind was troubled. Would she sully Angela with her company? Was she unfit for polite society? Did Lord Bryn sense how she felt, and was he offended by it? And how would she get through the days and nights of her life without him?

There was no use refining on matters she could not resolve. Instead, Meg had to confront a more immediate issue, the need to advise Helen Cockerell of her return without admitting the circumstances under which she had been living.

Or perhaps she did not have to keep up a pretence with her closest friend. Surely Helen would guess something was amiss if she did. It might be courting disaster to reveal to others that she had paraded as a governess, but Helen could be trusted. She would tell no one; she would even think it a lark.

London. Meg closed her eyes and it came back to her: the heavy perfumes of the ton, the sneers upon their lips, the crushes as one entered a ball, the sound of laughter behind one's back. Oh, Lord, was she really going back there?

Gowns! She had not even a dress suitable to wear in society, now that hers had been redone for Angela.

Meg hesitated to appeal to Helen. True, her friend possessed an enormous wardrobe and disliked wearing the same gown more than two or three times, and the two girls were close to the same size. Helen would likely not mind at all providing some gowns to be made over for Meg, but to make such a request, Meg must reveal the truly difficult state of their finances.

Well, Helen would scarcely be surprised. She was perceptive enough to have guessed the facts already.

With a frown, Meg picked up her pen and set to the difficult task of outlining her escapades, and her poverty, to the only person outside her family whom she dared trust with such information.

ON FRIDAY MORNING, Lord Bryn and Miss Geraint went riding together. Standing in the schoolroom window, Meg watched them go.

However gawky she might look on the ground, Germaine more than compensated for it with her horsemanship. She rode as if born to the saddle, Meg noted, as the figures galloped across a rise side by side.

Her own poor vision would never permit such activity, Meg reflected. Until now, she had thought the marquis and his future wife singularly ill-suited, but she was beginning to realize her error. Lord Bryn had chosen the life of a country gentlemen, and Germaine clearly was in accord with him. It mattered not that Meg liked the country life, also, despite the fact she missed her mother and sister. Feeling wretched, she returned to supervising the children.

Meg managed to keep her restless thoughts in check for the next few hours, but the sense of unease returned during her free hour while the children and the house guests napped. She had heard Lord Bryn go into his study some time ago, and felt she could safely walk about the grounds without risking an encounter.

There was nothing approaching a formal garden here. Rolling fields, thick with buttercups, surrounded the great house. Farther away, cattle moved across the grassy slopes. Meg paused to drink in the warm summer air and the rich earthy smell, and to wonder where she belonged. She would never have imagined, having taken such unwanted leave of her family in London, that she would feel pain at having to go back again.

Suddenly she needed to be alone, not wishing anyone to come out and witness her distress. Meg began walking almost aimlessly, until she reached a wooded ridge which afforded shelter from view. Here she sank onto a fallen trunk and wrapped her arms around her knees.

Was this really love she felt for the marquis? The poets wrote about such things in flowery terms, yet what Meg felt was far from flowery. It was confusing, painful, exciting, and terrifying. It made sense of the stories she had heard, of people doing foolish things, casting away their friends and reputations. But she could never go so far, not while her mother's and sister's futures hung in the balance.

"Are you ill?" She hadn't heard so much as a footstep, but there he was, standing over her like some giant from a legend, his voice thick with concern. "May I help you?"

"Oh . . . no." Meg's throat cramped drily against the words. "I . . . I was merely wool-gathering, my lord."

He sat beside her, folding his long legs without a trace of awkwardness. Although they did not touch, Meg could almost feel the log vibrate with his strength and energy. "We shall miss you here." There was none of the accustomed guardedness in his words.

"And I shall miss all of you." She rested her cheek against the top of her knees like a young girl. Being in his presence felt so natural that it was hard to remember the difference, however contrived, in their stations. "Miss Geraint is a fine woman. I admire her greatly."

"Of course." He passed over the topic without interest. "Do you get about much in London? I'm wondering if it has changed much during my absence."

"Tell me what it was like, and I'll tell you if it has changed," she said, "although I doubt I know the whereabouts of any of your acquaintances."

"It isn't the individuals who matter, is it?" The dark brooding look had returned to his eyes. "Only the frenzied chase of whatever is fashionable at the moment, the love of gossip, the waste of money and lives."

"Surely not everyone is so shallow." He had given a good description of the ton, but as Meg knew, there were dear faces and kind souls seen in the most stylish circles.

"So shallow? Oh, no, some fancy themselves deep and glorious." Bitterness coloured Lord Bryn's words, and she wondered at the intensity of it. "They dream of doing great deeds, of seeing their names writ in the history books."

"Is that a fault?" Nearby a bird twittered lazily in the summer air.

The marquis seemed to awaken from some momentary trance. "Real courage is no fault, of course, my dear, but vanity is a much underrated vice."

He seemed not to notice the endearment, and Meg pretended not to have heard it, but in her heart she cherished it. "Are you speaking of yourself, my lord?"

To her amazement the marquis buried his face in his hands, though only for a moment. When he lifted his head, his lips where white with strain. "Yes, I was such a peacock. I went off to war determined to make myself a hero. But it was someone else who paid the price, a devoted servant. Killed through my own carelessness in neglecting to send him to safety. I know my friends thought little of it— he was only a valet. But he was a man, the same as I. And he loved me dearly, a love I did not deserve."

Meg fought back the impulse to console him and tried instead to imagine her own feelings if Karen had somehow died due to her carelessness. She shivered. "If there were only some way to atone."

His hand closed over hers. It was a large hand, with a scar across the back, but very gentle. "I have learned to live with my guilt. That seems to be the best I can do."

They sat together in silence for a while, inhaling the sweetness of the earth's bounty. Meg felt closer to him even than when they had kissed. She knew then that, even if she never saw him again, he would always be a part of her.

"I'm sorry if I've been thoughtless of you." His grip tightened on her hand. "I had hoped, had the Geraints not come so early—" He stopped, perhaps realizing that propriety forbade him to confide further.

"You have done nothing wrong." With her last small reservoir of strength, Meg forced herself to stand and move away. "I must go and see to the children."

He rose beside her. "Yes. And I have accounts to tend."

"Wait." She caught her skirts in her hand. "We must not walk together. It wouldn't be seemly." Within her, a small voice shouted to throw away propriety, to beg him to keep her close always, to declare that she would never leave. What worlds they would shatter if they dared behave so outrageously! In the end, Meg knew with painful clarity, such selfishness could only come back on them and wreak a vengeance of its own. "Good day, my lord."

Stiffly she walked away into the sunshine and did not look back.

CHAPTER THIRTEEN

MEG EXAMINED HER GOWNS carefully, an easy task since she had brought only four.

The first, her brown gabardine, was out of the question, nor would her grey walking dress serve. The choice, then, was between the blue dress she had worn to Squire Roberts's house and a simple peach muslin.

For a moment, Meg pictured one of her London gowns, made-over and looking splendid on Angela. Beautiful, innocent Angela, dancing with Mr. Cockerell. What a pair the two of them must make, he tall and erect, she small and blonde and lively.

Meg thought of the letter she'd received that morning. Engaged! Who would ever have thought the man would be the stiff-necked Edward Cockerell?

As for herself, she doubted the marquis would condescend to dance with her tonight. If only one sister could be happy, she preferred that it be Angela; but wearing a fine dress to the ball might have at least soothed her pride.

Well, the peach would have to do, she decided, although it had a rip at the hem. Perhaps Mrs. Franklin would lend her needle and thread for mending.

Someone rapped firmly on the door.

"Come in," Meg called.

Germaine pushed the door open with her shoulder and strode into the room amid an armful of silks and velvets and satins in frothy colours.

"Oh, please, you needn't have brought your gowns! I should have been delighted to come to your room if you need any advice," said Meg, amused to find Miss Geraint was also having trouble selecting her attire.

"Nonsense." Germaine dumped the lot unceremoniously on the bed. "These ain't for me—they're for you."

"What?" Meg stared at her.

"Don't know as they'll fit," Germaine admitted, plumping herself beside the stack of dresses. "I'm a considerable bit taller than you. Broader, as well. But with a tuck here and there, one of them might do."

Meg flushed as she fingered the delicate fabrics, remembering that she'd been concerned about her effect on the marquis. And here was Germaine, trustingly offering to help! She resolved silently to bury her feelings for Lord Bryn, now and forever.

"You're too generous," she said at last.

"Not a bit of it." Germaine watched with evident gratification as Meg held one gown and then another against herself in the mirror. "Blooming waste of time, fancying me up in fine laces and velvets. You've seen at fairs how they braid up the horses' manes with flowers? That's how I feel at a ball."

"So do I—" Meg whirled around, holding a flow of seagreen silk to her "—without my lorgnette! Oh, Miss Geraint, you should have been there—" She bit her lip barely in time to stop a description of the evening at Almack's. "Well, I used to cut my best friends, simply from not seeing them," she finished lamely.

"You like that one, do you?" Germaine nodded approvingly. "Let's have a look at it on you, then."

Donning the dress, Meg stared into the mirror wonderingly.

The green intensified the blue of her eyes and set off the auburn highlights of her soft brown hair. Her skin appeared ivory pale and clear against the rich silk, and the scooped neckline and high waist accentuated her rounded bosom and slender figure.

She had never felt more than mildly pretty before. Was it only the gown that had wrought this change, or was it the depths of emotion she'd experienced for the first time here at Brynwood?

Within minutes, the women were occupied adjusting the gown to Meg's smaller frame. Fortunately it was of simple design and, as Germaine had predicted, a few tucks and a raised hem sufficed—at least here in the country, where Meg wouldn't be scrutinized as she would have been in town.

Later that evening Meg ate a quiet supper in her room, declining an invitation to join the family at dinner. She didn't want the marquis to see her in this flattering dress, for fear of playing upon the passions he had already evidenced. The result could only be extremely painful to everyone. And might it not further inflame those shocking tendencies she had discovered in herself, those yearnings that no decent woman should feel?

Although there had been no announcement, she knew tonight was intended as an engagement ball. Curiously Lord Bryn had shown no special attention to Miss Geraint, at least not as far as Meg could tell.

Could the reason be his own uncertainty about the match? After the closeness she and the marquis had shared on Thursday afternoon, she surmised that he had come to care for her at least a little. But he had a duty to Germaine, and it must be fulfilled. If he scorned the lady now, the result would be Germaine's humiliation and the end of her hopes for a marriage.

So Meg determined to remain in her room until most of the guests had arrived. She even considered putting aside the new dress for her old peach one, but Germaine might possibly be offended. Or Meg could plead a headache and avoid the ball entirely. But Miss Geraint would be certain to come up and investigate.

She would simply go down and blend into the crowd, Meg thought. The marquis had been properly distant the past two days; no doubt, to soothe her own heartache, she was simply imagining that he favoured her.

There was one audience whose attention she didn't mind attracting. As the strains of the small orchestra wafted up the stairs, Meg darted into the nursery to show her dress to the children.

"Miss Linley!" For once Vanessa was struck dumb, staring in awe at the shining lady in green.

"You look like an angel!" declared Tom, sitting up in bed. "Uncle Andrew's certain to marry you!"

"Don't be foolish," said Meg. "He's going to wed Miss Geraint, and a good thing, too. She'll keep the pair of you in line, and she's a fine horsewoman."

"I want to grow up like you," said Vanessa softly.

Meg kissed them both and tucked them back in. "I shall miss you terribly when I leave. If I write, will you write back?"

"Of course," said Vanessa. "I shall write for Tom, too, until he learns how."

Meg hurried away to hide the brimming tears.

The ballroom, aired and cleaned after a long hibernation, glowed with the light of hundreds of candles arrayed in sconces along the wall. Potted ferns and orange trees had been placed artfully about, screening the refreshment tables and the hovering servants. Meg paused, unobserved, to watch the assembly.

Lord Bryn was standing up with Miss Geraint to the strains of a quadrille. The lady performed the stylized dance without the least pretence of grace. Indeed, Germaine looked as though she heartily wished there were a fence to leap or a fox to pursue.

The marquis bowed politely as the music ended, and escorted his companion to the side for a glass of ratafia, which she downed in a single gulp. It was then that he turned and caught sight of Meg.

The noisy ballroom faded away. He had been preparing himself all evening for the sight of her, only to find that his precautions had failed to arm his heart. She was radiantly beautiful, more so than he had imagined possible. Vaguely he noted the striking colour of her gown, but he had little interest in fashion. It was her face that held him, the eyes widening as they met his, the lips soft and full.

Then she looked away. A straightening of the shoulders, a toss of the head hinted at that inner strength he already knew.

A voice near at hand recalled the marquis to himself. Ah, yes, Squire Roberts, asking for a dance with Miss Geraint. Andrew yielded graciously, hoping the poor girl wouldn't be bored to death with the man's talk of horses and hunts.

Bryn would take Mr. Geraint aside later tonight and request his consent to a match, and then put the matter to the lady. He should have done so earlier in the visit, yet there had seemed always to be some matter requiring his attention, and the hours had passed before he knew it. Well, there would be plenty of time to arrange the betrothal and announce it before the midnight supper. Certainly the request was little more than a formality, since his man of affairs had already been treating with Mr. Geraint on a marriage settlement.

Lord Bryn took a sip of Madeira. He knew he must not attend on Miss Linley, or his best efforts would be lost. How he had come to lose his heart to a governess, he could not have said. The marquis was no snob, and had he been free, he would have asked for her hand.

Indeed, on Thursday he had cherished the hope that the matter of Miss Geraint might be resolved without public embarrassment. He could have sent a note round to the inn where the family was to have stayed. They need only have turned back, telling the world any story they liked. Although his intentions were well-known, the marquis hadn't yet formally asked to marry Miss Geraint, and scandal could have been avoided had she called off their visit.

But they had arrived early—it seemed Mrs. Geraint, weary of being on the road, had hastened their progress—and once they reached his home their agreement to the match became evident. For a gentleman to throw over a lady was to sully her reputation, for it was generally assumed that he must have been given strong reason to do so.

Therefore he must not speak with Miss Linley before her departure, must scarcely acknowledge her save as a member of his staff, must pretend that he felt nothing for her. Did she guess? Did she ever feel the same for him, or had she merely acquiesced to his embrace out of fear or respect?

In any event, propriety required that he avoid her, for once in her arms upon the dance floor, Andrew knew he could never free himself again.

Impulsively, he sought out Mr. Geraint and they went to the study. There, with apologies for the delay, Andrew made his request.

"Certainly you have my permission, Lord Bryn." It was the longest speech he'd ever heard from the taciturn man. "But winning my Geri's heart, that's another story."

The marquis almost choked on his wine, but managed to maintain an earnest expression. The two men walked companionably back to the ballroom, where Andrew stood watching his guests and feeling uncomfortably like one side of a highly irregular triangle.

Had he but known it, there was another such construction at Brynwood that night. It concerned Miss Conley, Miss Ludden and Mr. Jeffrey Roberts.

Miss Conley, who had considered herself rusticating when she came from Liverpool to visit her elderly great-aunts, was a sought-after Beauty at home. Therefore she found it all the more difficult to understand why Mr. Roberts, the only eligible young man at the ball, was busying himself with Miss Ludden, a great gawk of a girl. Indeed, he had danced with Miss Conley only once, and with Miss Ludden three times. Intolerable!

When the music ended, Miss Conley made her way to the young man and smiled up at him warmly, although she would have liked to slap his weak-chinned face. "I must have made a mistake," she murmured. "Did you not promise me the dance just past? I had written your name on my dance card." She produced the document and fluttered it beneath his nose.

"Did I?" Jeffrey turned a vivid red which went all the way to his ears. "I'm terribly sorry. Will the next dance do instead?"

"I suppose it must," said Miss Conley, sighing.

Thereafter, she kept the fellow busy with one assignment after another: more lemonade, a sugary French fruit, a walk on the balcony to enjoy the fresh air. By the time she slipped her hand daringly into his and kissed his cheek, the man had forgotten the very existence of the curate's daughter.

Miss Ludden sought the counsel of Miss Linley, who was only too glad of the distraction. The excitement of viewing the assembly through her quizzing glass had worn off the moment she witnessed Lord Bryn and Mr. Geraint leaving the room together.

Veronica explained her difficulty and added, "There is Squire Roberts attending Miss Geraint. If you could demonstrate on them how to win a man away..."

"I'm afraid it wouldn't be the same," said Meg. "Miss Geraint is going to marry Lord Bryn. She has no interest in the squire."

The girl frowned. "Then why is she enjoying her conversation with the squire so much?"

Meg followed her gaze. Germaine and Squire Roberts stood to one side, engaged in a lively discussion that, from the gestures, could only have been about fox hunting.

"They have a great deal in common," she explained.

"Well?" Veronica stared up hopefully. "Can't you help me? I'm at my wit's end, Miss Linley."

"We shall see." Reluctantly Meg led the way to the animated couple, arriving at almost the same time as the marquis.

There they stood, the five of them: Veronica anxiously awaiting her instruction, Meg and Lord Bryn trying to avoid each other's eyes and Germaine and Squire Roberts discoursing heatedly as to whether it was unsportsmanlike to use bag foxes if none could be spotted running free.

Aware of her responsibilities to Miss Ludden and feeling confident that Germaine wouldn't mind disposing of this extra gentleman, Meg offered her own opinion and joined the discussion.

The squire appeared highly amused at this sally from such a delicate chit, who had obviously never ridden in a fox hunt, and he patted her shoulder.

A pretty lass, he told himself, but she couldn't compare with Miss Geraint. That was a woman who could keep him in line. He'd warrant she'd take a whip to him if need be when drink caused him to lose his temper. The marquis, he decided, was a lucky devil.

Lord Bryn's thoughts were centred on Meg. How dared the bounder lay his hand upon her? No doubt he thought a mere governess fair game for his tricks. Or he meant to make her his wife, little better than a servant and a whipping boy!

No one but Meg noticed when Veronica slipped away. She observed through the crowd how the girl walked up to Jeffrey and Miss Conley and joined their chatter directly, and how a few minutes later the young man was dancing once again with Miss Ludden.

As for Miss Conley, she might yet have prevailed, for she had a great advantage in beauty, but she stalked off in a fury and paid no more heed to the younger Mr. Roberts for the rest of the evening.

In the meantime, Germaine was growing more and more displeased that no one was dancing with Meg, for she had developed a protective feeling about the vulnerable young governess. Furthermore, she took pride in the transformation wrought by the green gown upon her protégée, and wondered why the gentlemen weren't being more attentive.

She briefly considered prevailing upon the squire to ask Meg for a dance, but he was far and away the most interesting man she had met in some time. Instead she turned to the marquis. "Lord Bryn, don't stand about looking hangdog. Dance with Miss Linley!"

His lordship appeared taken aback, but she'd left him no choice. With a stiff bow, he made the request of Miss Linley, and she agreed before she realized the orchestra was beginning a waltz. She had hoped for a less intimate Scottish reel.

Her heart fluttered as they walked out together and he placed one hand upon her waist. Meg felt herself blushing fiercely.

"You look splendid tonight, Miss Linley," the marquis murmured.

"Thank you." She dared to look up at him, trying to store away the sight of his beloved face for the long years ahead. "It was kind of Miss Geraint to lend me her gown."

They moved easily together, palm against palm. Meg longed to run her hand across the superfine of his coat, to press her cheek to his shoulder.

Nor was his lordship immune to the lady's appeal. He wanted her in a way he had never experienced before. The scent of her was intoxicating, although he could discern no particular perfume. A subtly alluring fragrance wafted up from her hair and skin, filling his veins like an intoxicating liquor, tempting but never satisfying, so that he wanted all of her and knew even that would scarcely be enough.

For the first time in his life, the marquis understood the crazy things some people did. Men running off with milkmaids, ladies marrying their butlers, couples dashing away to Scotland in defiance of their parents.

So this was love, he thought. And he had found it too late.

For the brief spell of the dance, they were lost in a world together, but then it ended. Drawing with difficulty upon his sense of duty, the marquis relinquished Miss Linley and gazed about for Miss Geraint.

Where the devil was she?

In fact, she was at that moment walking on the balcony with Squire Roberts, discussing the breeding of mares.

"I say," the squire remarked at last, "you don't find this matter a bit, er, vulgar? I've no wish to offend."

"Stuff and nonsense," replied Germaine. "What else is there worth talking about? Anyone who worries about offending me is wasting his time, for I've a stronger stomach than most *men* of my acquaintance."

"That I'll vouch for!" agreed the squire, who had watched the lady down three glasses of sherry in the past half hour. Not only a hunting companion, but a drinking partner! "Well, if you promise not to take offence, what do you say to marrying me instead of his lordship?"

"Done," said Germaine.

"Beg pardon?"

"Done," she repeated. "You've got yourself a wife."

"Well, bless my— You don't say! Damnedest thing!" Finally recalled to propriety, Squire Roberts went off to find Mr. Geraint and ask his blessing.

It was then that Lord Bryn discovered Germaine alone just inside the terrace doors. There would never be a better time, he reflected. "Miss Geraint?" he said. "May I speak with you privately?"

She cast a peculiar look at him but nodded and stepped outside. The marquis cleared his throat. Now that the moment had come, doubts assailed him. More than doubts; certainties. But he must carry on.

"You surely are aware of why you and your family were invited here," said Lord Bryn. "I, er, wish to ask for your hand in marriage."

"Too late!" boomed Germaine. "Already promised myself to Squire Roberts. You need a more direct manner if you're to capture a lady's heart, Lord Bryn." She clapped him on the shoulder and strode back into the ballroom.

Andrew stood there openmouthed, staring after her.

Then he went in search of Miss Linley.

CHAPTER FOURTEEN

MEG COULD SCARCELY BELIEVE it when the marquis appeared at her side and asked to speak with her privately.

Whatever could be the matter? She glanced worriedly at Germaine, but that lady only smiled broadly and winked. Beyond her, on the balcony, Squire Roberts and Mr. Geraint were conducting an earnest conversation.

In a daze, Meg laid her hand on Lord Bryn's arm and accompanied him to his study. She'd imagined such a scene a hundred times, but the marquis couldn't possibly intend what she'd dreamed.

He closed the door behind them, a most improper thing to do. What did it mean? "Sherry?" The marquis offered her a glass and, with a weak nod, Meg sank onto the settee.

"Have I done something wrong?" she asked.

"Not at all." He handed her the liquid and she swallowed a gulp, nearly coughing at the unaccustomed fire of it.

The marquis moved around his desk and sat on its edge. "How would you like to bring your mother to live at Brynwood?"

"My mother? Here?" Meg couldn't think straight. How handsome he looked in the glow of the lamp. Why did he watch her so intently? She had to think of some excuse about her mother....

"That's my roundabout way of proposing marriage." Lord Bryn gave a small, self-deprecating smile. "I realize I haven't done it properly. You've no father to ask, I gather, and I've no acquaintance with your mother. So I put the matter to you directly."

"But, Miss Geraint . . . ?"

"She has been stolen from under my very nose, and by none other than Squire Roberts." He spoke with dry irony.

"They're going to be married?"

"So she tells me." He stared down into his glass, then looked up. "Well, Miss Linley? Do you choose to become Lady Bryn?"

Meg couldn't believe this was true. He hadn't said he loved her, but why else would he make such an offer? "My answer will be yes," she said, "but first I must make an explanation."

"I hardly think it can be so important as all that." The marquis crossed the room to sit beside her, slipping one arm about her waist.

"We must be honest with each other," Meg protested. "I shall feel much better when we've laid our cards upon the table."

"Let's not talk of gambling at such a time, shall we?" he teased.

Before she could reply, his mouth closed over hers. A thousand stars swirled through Meg's mind and, dizzied, she leaned against the marquis for support. He held her firmly, his lips exploring her cheeks and eyelids and brow.

All awareness of place and time dissolved. Nothing existed for Meg but the warmth of his mouth, lifting her out of this earthly realm. The two of them were flung among the heavens, far-off lights dancing about them. They were dancing themselves, to distant music, moving against each other gently and then with growing intensity.

His grip on her tightened, and his lips traced the delicate curve of her throat, down to the soft white expanse of bosom exposed by the fashionable gown. Shivers of desire ran through Meg, and she understood in one blinding instant what it was she longed for and why in a moment she would no longer be able to resist.

"My lord," she gasped with her last ounce of resolve. "We are not yet married."

"I cannot bear to wait much longer." With a harsh intake of breath, the marquis released her and turned away, his shoulders tense as he fought for control. "I shall request the curate to marry us as soon as possible. Damn the formalities."

Before Meg could respond, there came a knock at the door. Muttering a curse, the lordship strode angrily across the room. "Yes?"

It was Franklin. "My lord, forgive me for interrupting you." He maintained an impassive air which masked any surprise at the sight of Meg standing there breathless and somewhat disheveled. "Two rough fellows have turned up demanding to see, er, a certain person in the household."

Lord Bryn frowned in annoyance. "Well, deal with them as you see best. I have more important matters to tend to."

Franklin hesitated. "May I have a word with you in private, my lord?"

For a moment, the marquis looked as though he might refuse, but then he said shortly, "Very well," and stepped into the hallway.

Left alone, Meg tried to sort out her emotions. Her body burned from his touch, and she knew it was dangerous to delay their marriage, for they were not in full control of their passions. Yet she couldn't marry without her mother and sister present. And there still remained the necessity of telling Lord Bryn the truth about herself.

The thought was like a dash of cold water. How would he respond? Surely if he loved her he would forgive such an innocent deception. Or would he?

In the hallway the marquis was also having a difficult time, not so much with his sentiments as with the bizarre tale Franklin was recounting.

"A pair of drunkards? Asking for Miss Linley? Nonsense!" He took care to keep his tone low. "Let me speak with them."

Franklin led the way to the kitchen, where two scragglylooking men lolled before the fire, their cheeks and noses scarlet from the combined effects of drink and heat.

"I wish to be alone with these men," Lord Bryn commanded. "Franklin may remain."

He waited as the other servants departed, since he had no wish for idle tongues to repeat whatever calumnies these ne'er-do-wells might spread about Miss Linley. "Well?" he demanded. "What is this story you've told my butler?"

"Ain't no story," said the smaller of the pair, whom Franklin identified as Fred Coves. "We heard from the family she was comin' to work here and thought it was time we paid her a visit."

"She's our cousin," added his companion, who was known as Artie. "No harm in coming to see our cousin, is there? Thought she'd show us around a bit, fancy house and all."

"I believe they're salt miners from Northwich way," Franklin interposed. "In spite of their demeanour, my lord, there's no reason to doubt their relationship."

Relationship? These ruffians, cousins to his Meg? The prospect of becoming a cousin-by-marriage to these rogues was dismaying, but the marquis suspected they would be easily got rid of—for a time, at least. "And you've come purely from motives of good fellowship, is it?" The fellows exchanged looks. A narrowing of the eye, a quirk of the lip told the marquis all he needed to know. "Or to intimidate her into bribing you to leave? Is that it?"

A sneer revealed Fred's rotting front teeth. "We're askin' nothin'. She be our cousin, that's all."

Meg wasn't the sort to let herself be pushed around, Bryn reflected. Time to throw these scoundrels out. "We'll let her speak for herself, then."

He flung open the door, nearly tumbling in the servants who had crowded there to listen. They started back apologetically, and at his order, one of the maids ran to summon Miss Linley from the study.

A few minutes later he heard her footsteps approaching. Odd how he could have picked that soft footfall out of a crowd. "Yes, my lord?" She stepped into the room, looking every bit as lovely as she had only moments ago in his arms.

"Do you know these men?" he asked impatiently. "They've come to see their cousin. Have you anything to say to them?"

"What, her?" snarled the fellow known as Fred. "That ain't Myra. She's an impostor! What's she done with your governess, that's what I'd like to know!"

Meg's face turned an unnatural white, and then she swooned.

CHAPTER FIFTEEN

MEG AWOKE to find herself still in the kitchen, half-sprawled in a chair and being fanned by Mrs. Franklin. The two nasty-looking men sat staring at her in dismay, and she gathered that only a minute or two had passed.

"That ain't Myra!" declared Artie, turning to his companion. "Eh, Fred?"

The other fellow nodded. "Don't even have the look of a Lindsay. Though faintin', well, that's somethin' Myra does a lot."

"Well, Meg." The marquis regarded her with narrowed eyes. "What have you done with Myra Lindsay, and who in heaven's name are you?"

Meg wished devoutly at that moment that the floor would open up and swallow her. Again and again over the past few weeks she had tried to envision the scene in which she would reveal the truth to the marquis. Never had she imagined, even in her harshest dreams, that the revelation would be made at such an awkward time and in the most embarrassing of circumstances, certain to make her actions appear in the worst possible light.

"I'm Margaret Linley," she whispered. "I'm...not really a governess. The real Myra Lindsay was on the mail with me from London. She was mistakenly accused of theft, and had hysterics. Even though the purse was found, she insisted on turning back."

A spell of silence elapsed while everyone in the room digested this information. Coldness edged the marquis's voice when he spoke at last. "Interesting. However, it fails to explain your presence here."

Vaguely Meg became aware that others had entered the room. She caught a glimpse of Germaine, Squire Roberts, and other guests, as well as servants. There was no avoiding an answer, although she dearly wished the marquis would interview her in private. But from the hardness of his expression, she could expect no mercy.

"I was travelling from London to Derby with my maidservant," she said. "She was to arrange my transportation from Manchester and then make her own way to Liverpool, to be married."

"Never heard of such a thing." Mrs. Geraint sniffed. "I'd have given her the sack!"

Meg ignored this remark. "I was in my private salon, awaiting the driver from the post chaise, when a coachman came to the door inquiring about Miss Lindsay. I assumed he meant me. I'm so nearsighted that I didn't recognize the carriage for a private one." Intense silence radiated from her listeners like pine scent from a Christmas tree. "I was brought here, to Brynwood, where I encountered your lordship and the children and discovered I had been mistaken for a governess."

"And you thought it would be a great sport to pretend that you really were Miss Lindsay?" Disgust hardened the marquis's features to a mask. "A lark to entertain your friends when you go back to London?"

How to explain what she couldn't justify even to herself? "No! It wasn't at all like that! I…I haven't any plans to go back to town. I liked the children very much and I enjoyed feeling useful…."

How weak her words sounded to her own ears, and how wintry and distant the marquis looked. "You told me all this in jest, I recall. That must have increased your amusement, to pretend to tell me the truth and joke with me about it. What a fine on-dit that will make among your silly friends.''

Had he ceased to love her so thoroughly that he could now suspect her of almost unlimited wrongdoing? "I'm not so low as that!" she retorted. "I have no use for cruel gossip. My mother is Lady Mary Linley, and I am a good friend, as it happens, of Miss Geraint's cousins, Helen and Edward Cockerell. Indeed, they were kind enough to sponsor my sister, Angela, at her come-out."

"Quite right, Helen's mentioned you in her letters!" cried Germaine. "Good show! Getting on the wrong carriage. Bully for you, sticking it out! Been a good governess, too, and not many ladies could handle that job. Knew from the first that you was quality."

"Disgraceful carryings-on," muttered Mrs. Geraint.

"Let the girl be," said her husband. "Rousing good story."

"Kind of thing the ton is always doing, ain't it?" said Squire Roberts. "Going about having a lark? Don't see no point in taking on about it. No harm done."

There was much nodding around the room, and a general sense of relief that Meg Linley had turned out to be respectable after all. With that, the crowd dispersed, returning to their respective activities.

Fred and Artie eyed Meg speculatively, as if debating whether or not there was some way to turn this situation to advantage. Any plans they might have hatched were cut short when Franklin handed them each a packet of food and escorted them firmly to the back door. After they departed, the butler discreetly made his own exit into the hallway, leaving the two principals alone.

Meg stared up at the marquis, hope dying at the revulsion she saw on his face. "Please believe I never meant you any harm. I am not the kind of thistle-brain you believe me, my lord."

He turned on his heel and stalked away.

After a stunned moment, Meg retreated, shaken, to her room. Standing before the mirror, she removed the sea-green silk, her fingers smoothing the soft material. How beautiful it had seemed before, and how she hated the sight of it now. The most splendid evening of her life had ended in disaster. All her self-justification and excuses had come to naught. She had been exposed in the most humiliating manner possible.

Why did it have to happen just when she was on the verge of the greatest happiness of her life? Tears slid unchecked down Meg's face as she recalled the tenderness in Lord Bryn's eyes when he proposed to her. Then she burned with shame, recalling the wanton manner in which she had allowed herself to be caressed.

He could ruin her forever, her and her family, if he chose to make common gossip of her conduct. As for her heart, it remained his possession to cast into the dustheap if he wished. Falling across the bed in her cambric slip, Meg buried her face in her arms and wept.

A rustling at the door announced Germaine's arrival. The woman sank onto the bed and stroked Meg's hair sympathetically. "Bravely done," she declared. "No harm in a bit of a prank."

"Andrew will never forgive me." Meg tasted his dear name on her lips, salty and bitter. "You must believe, I never intended a prank. It was my own weakness that kept me here, but he refuses to see it."

"Damn fool!" said Germaine. "He's fallen in love with you, ain't he? No, don't bother denying it. I have eyes in my head. Would he have preferred that you'd gone on about your business? It was a rare stroke of luck, your landing here by mistake and not stalking off in a huff. Anyone else would claim they'd been kidnapped!"

"Do you think he might calm down by morning?" Meg asked without much hope.

"If he's got any sense, he will." Germaine kicked off her shoes and they hit the wall with a thump. "Men are such fools. Even Squire Roberts. But he's a bit of all right, anyway."

"Do you suppose word of this will get back to London?" Meg asked. "I don't mind so much for myself—I'm already in disgrace. But my sister—"

"No one will hear of it from my family," Germaine assured her. "And I doubt his lordship will want this awkwardness bruited about. He'll lecture his servants soundly on the matter of keeping quiet."

Meg lay awake for a long time after her friend left, until the music ended downstairs and she heard carriages rattle away through the night. Some of the guests were staying until morning, and she heard them rustling and laughing as they went to their rooms.

The next day, she breakfasted in her room and waited. The summons from the marquis didn't come until the overnight guests had departed. Then, at a word from Mrs. Franklin, Meg trailed reluctantly down to his lordship's study, which held such tormenting memories from the previous night.

Lord Bryn remained seated behind his desk as she entered. His face looked thin and stretched, as though he hadn't slept.

Meg paused in the doorway, longing to reach out to him. "My lord—"

"Be seated, Miss Linley." There was no friendliness in the tone.

She perched on a chair, ignoring the settee. "I know I've done wrong, but it was always my intention to tell you the truth. I meant to, that night Miss Geraint arrived, and again yesterday before I—" She couldn't bring herself to say "accepted your proposal" and so finished, "before I gave you my answer."

"I have devoted some thought to this matter." The marquis closed his eyes for a moment, as if to gain better control of himself. "I realize that from your point of view, as Squire Roberts said, your conduct constitutes nothing more than a lark of the sort so popular among the ton."

"Not at all—"

"I'm not finished." The words rapped out with harsh authority. "I believe it would be best for both of us if nothing more were said of this unfortunate incident, nor of any of its ramifications."

Including his proposal of marriage. Meg stared at Lord Bryn in misery.

Taking her silence for assent, he continued, "I will arrange for you to be driven to Manchester tomorrow, where you may take the mail to wherever you please. We shall return you to where we claimed you. Does that satisfy you, Miss Linley?"

Her hands clenched into fists of tension. "There are other matters I wish to discuss before I depart, Lord Bryn."

He shifted, looking ill at ease. "Naturally, in the light of these revelations, you cannot expect me to honour the offer I made to you last night."

"No, I don't hold you to that." As she spoke, Meg tried to store up every detail of his face, the way the light from the window played across his high cheekbones, the slight irregularity which gave his nose distinction, the deep brown of his eyes. Must she be content with only memories the rest of her days?

"What do you wish to say?"

"First, I would appreciate it if the children weren't advised of this development," Meg said. "They already know that I'm leaving, and it might upset them unnecessarily."

"Very well," said the marquis.

"And, my lord—" she leaned forward, desperation forcing her to wrench the words from her heart "—I made no pretence when I told you my sentiments last night. My feelings toward you haven't changed."

"Mine have," he replied.

"I cannot believe that!" She caught hold of the chair arms to keep herself from leaping up. "You can have cared little for me to have changed so quickly, and I do not believe you would have proposed to a governess if you didn't care for her a great deal!"

"You presume too much, Miss Linley," he snapped.

"I love you!" The cry came from Meg's heart. "I think I loved you from the start, and that's why I stayed!"

"Is this another of your cruel jests?" Fury blazed across his face. "You have no intention of keeping your success a secret, have you, Miss Linley?"

"What can you mean?"

"My proposal is to be made sport of in the drawing rooms of London, is it not?" He stood and gripped the edge of the desk until his knuckles whitened. "What a tale you shall have to amuse your frivolous companions!"

"I would never dream of such a thing!" She jumped to her feet, furious that he would misconstrue her actions.

"You shall continue your journey to Derby, then?" he inquired.

"No," she admitted. "My mother writes that I may return to London. I left because of a minor scandal—I cut Beau Brummell, because I failed to see him."

"Serves the jumped-up popinjay right." A ghost of a smile vanished quickly. "Was that another of your tricks?"

"I think you misunderstand me willfully!" She glared at him. Never had she dreamed the man could be so impossible!

"Allow me to explain something to you, Miss Linley." There was no longer even a hint of warmth. "I abandoned society because I could no longer tolerate its emptiness and its selfishness. It is precisely to avoid young ladies like yourself that I've remained in the country these past two years."

"You didn't wish to avoid me yesterday!" she retorted before she could stop herself.

"There's no need to remind me of my folly." What a stranger he had become, this tall, angry man. "In any event, I will honour my word by saying nothing about this affair. If you choose to make it one of your on-dits, however, I assure you I shall reconsider. It wouldn't do your reputation any good to have certain matters spread about, would it?" His gaze trailed meaningfully down to the collar of Meg's gabardine dress, and her body flamed at the memory of their passionate embrace the previous night.

She gasped. "You'd do such a thing?"

"Only if you're the first to speak." A thin smile touched his face—not of happiness but of satisfaction. He was convinced that she meant to make sport of him, that she had trifled with his affections. How could she ever persuade him otherwise?

Meg stood in a ray of late-morning sunlight, trying to think of a way to plead her case. To argue, beg, threaten, say anything to break through this wall he'd thrown up between them. Before entering the study, she'd vowed not to leave until she'd reawakened his affections. But she had declared her love and he had only twisted her words back on her.

Gazing into his unrelenting eyes, she knew that she had lost.

"I'll say nothing, nor had I planned to, my lord," she replied. "You have a false opinion of me, but I see there is nothing I can do to correct it. If you should change your mind, I will leave my direction with Mrs. Franklin."

"You may do so if you wish," he said. "But you will not correspond with the children, Miss Linley. I don't care to have them exposed to someone of your character."

She would have thrown something at him then, but nothing came to hand. Instead she turned and stalked out the door.

Someone of her character! She would write to the children as she'd promised, and if the marquis wished to intercept the letters, at least she'd know she'd done her best.

Anger propelled Meg all the way back to her room, and then she burst into tears.

CHAPTER SIXTEEN

IRONICALLY IT WAS NOT Lady Darnet who succeeded in creating trouble for Angela. It was, unintentionally, Helen.

She was deeply fond of her young cousins, who were visiting the Cockerell household, but Rachel at age twelve had developed an obsession with society and its ways. The child pestered Helen from morning till night with questions. When could she toss aside her round kerseymere frocks for satin and sarcenet? Did she have to wait until eighteen to have her come-out? The youngster whined and pleaded for consent to try on Helen's clothes, or chattered for hours about the fashions in *La Belle Assemblée* and *The Lady's Magazine.*

There was only one room in the house into which the girl was not permitted to follow her, and that was Edward's study. So, when he was away from home, Helen developed the custom of retreating there to write her letters and read novels. She was careful to remove all her possessions each time, and Edward gave no sign of noticing.

It was there that Helen took refuge on Monday when she received an unusually long letter from Meg, and sat digesting its contents with growing amazement. Meg mistaken for a governess, and by Lord Bryn! What a delightful, if shocking, story. Helen had never had a friend half so interesting before.

She was pleased to see that her bosom bow was coming back to London. How unfortunate that Meg's gowns had been made over for Angela; of course Helen would be glad to spare some.

It was at this point that the butler rapped politely on the door and informed her there were visitors in the morning room.

Helen tucked the letter into her book, and then realized the problem. If she placed it downstairs in the house, Rachel would discover it. She had a bad habit of reading Helen's letters, and repeated scoldings had failed to have effect.

Not wanting to keep her guests waiting while she ran up to her bedchamber, Helen laid the volume on one of the low bookshelves where it would go unnoticed and she could re-claim it later. What she failed to observe, as she hurried out of the room, was that the hem of her skirt brushed against the book, tumbling it onto the carpet so that the letter fell free.

There it lay when Edward returned home a quarter of an hour later. He made a point of avoiding the morning room, as his marriage preparations left scant time for idle chit-chat. In fact, he had just come from discussing the ar-rangements with Lady Mary. She planned an engagement ball at her home at the end of the week, and had informed him happily that almost all of the invitations had been ac-cepted. For his part, Edward would have been gravely of-fended and surprised had his friends declined.

They had also dealt, perfunctorily, with the matter of the marriage portion and Angela's dowry. She had a respect-able if not overlarge one, left in trust by her grandfather before the war raised prices. Fortunately Edward didn't need the money; it was only that a girl of good family was expected to bring into marriage some funds of her own.

The actual ceremony was to take place in two weeks' time, allowing for the banns to be read. Edward hadn't been overly gratified to learn that the elder sister was returning to

London, but he had been assured that she would remain a demure figure in the background.

He wished, as he pushed open the door to his study, that there did not remain one small niggling doubt. It derived, he knew, from the conviction learned in childhood that one's duty and one's pleasure never coincided. It didn't seem possible that he could marry the charming, lovely, sweet Angela and meet his familial obligations at the same time. But what could possibly go wrong?

Edward's eye fell upon the displaced book and the letter. He frowned, then stooped to investigate.

The novel, he saw from the title, must be Helen's. As for the sheets of paper covered with writing, they might have blown onto the floor from his desk. Perhaps one of the maids had opened the window while cleaning.

Edward picked up the letter. Phrases leaped up at him. "Mistaken for a governess...this deception...return to London." And the signature. "Meg Linley."

With a sensation of dread, Edward sank onto a chair and began to read.

LADY DARNET WAS in a foul mood, and she saw no reason to moderate her temper in the presence of her cousin.

"The ball can mean only one thing!" She kicked viciously at the leg of a Chippendale chair. "They plan to announce their engagement!"

Sir Manfred was none too pleased by this observation, for his own reasons. "I cannot credit it, Cynthia. The chit has gone riding with me half a dozen times. I saw no sign of any courtship by Mr. Cockerell, although he did visit with his sister."

"Nevertheless, a marriage is afoot. Why did you not expose her sooner, you green goose?" The countess glared daggers at him.

"Expose? Ah, yes." The baronet had almost forgotten their original scheme to place Angela in a humiliating situation. It began to appeal to him again. Had she not placed him in a position of some embarrassment, accepting his attentions while setting her cap for another man?

"You must contrive something." Anger turned Lady Darnet's features into a hard mask. "At once! While there is still time for Edward to call it off."

"Yes, I shall devote some thought to it." Sir Manfred poured himself a glass of sherry. He was not given to rapid action, particularly when one might contemplate one's course over a glass of something or other.

"Some thought?" She smashed one fist upon a mahogany tea table, clattering the cups and saucers. When Cynthia was angry, it was often the furniture that suffered. "Today, I tell you! It must be done immediately!"

"There's no guarantee the fellow will throw himself at your head, even if he calls it off with Angela." The baronet watched cautiously to see if his cousin was about to launch another assault upon some hapless piece of the woodworker's art.

However, Lady Darnet confined her response to a small, rather nasty smile. "I know how to bring a gentleman round. Or force his hand if necessary. See that you do the same with that girl!"

This was outside of enough, Sir Manfred reflected as he finished his sherry. He might have told Cynthia to shake her skirts elsewhere but for his annoyance with Angela. If there was one thing he could not bear, it was to be made a fool of.

"I shall call upon her now." He set aside his glass. "And I expect you, dear cousin, to arrive half an hour later."

ANGELA WAS SURPRISED but happy to learn that her fiancé had returned scarcely more than an hour after he departed.

She flew past the butler on her way to the parlour and burst in, her face glowing with welcome. "Edward! What a delightful surprise!" Only then did she notice the scowl which lay heavily across his fair features. "Whatever is the matter?"

In response, he held out a letter. Angela took it, trying to quiet the trembling in her hands. She recognized the handwriting at once. Meg's. A letter to Helen.

It took only a swift perusal to confirm what she feared. "Edward—"

"Did you know of this?" he demanded.

"She wrote to us only this week." Angela hesitated. "I know it looks scandalous, but—"

He spoke as if he hadn't heard. "And is your family so badly dipped that they in truth cannot afford gowns for both sisters at once, and she must go begging to her friends?"

Angela felt the blood drain from her face. "We are not so well off as some might think, but my dowry is intact."

"There was a rumour—a lie, I'd thought it—that you were wearing your sister's made-over gown to the Opera." Edward might have been carved from wood for all the note he took of her distress. "Fool that I am, I defended you. So outrageous did I think the story that I lied to Lady Jersey and told her Helen had accompanied you to the dressmaker."

"I regret you were put in such an awkward position." Angela didn't know how to reach him; she could only wait while the storm played itself out.

"So I find that I have been cheated and deceived," Edward continued. "The woman I thought was an innocent young girl has been revealed as a schemer, interested in my money rather than my person."

"Edward!" Angela's hand flew to her mouth. "That's not true!"

"You are totally unsuitable to be my wife and to live with my family. I can only attribute Helen's complicity to the undue influence you and your sister wield over her."

"Helen has a kind heart!" Angela cried. "And as for you, Mr. Cockerell, you are seeing plots where none exist."

"You're an artful liar," he pressed on. "You persuaded me in spite of the evidence of my own eyes that your sister was blameless in the matter of Mr. Brummell."

"She was!"

"And in the question of Lord Bryn, as well?" He stood his ground, unmoved and unmoving. "I will be interested to hear how you explain away her intolerable behaviour. Your entire family is a disgrace."

She could bear it no longer. This pompous swell was insulting not only Angela but the mother and sister she loved more dearly than life itself.

"Get out!" She wished she had some item of china to throw at him. "Our engagement is at an end!"

"Indeed it is." He nodded in grim satisfaction. "So your schemes have been found out, and you play the self-righteous lady. Well, I will do this much for you, Miss Angela. Because my sister's reputation might also be harmed, I will say nothing of this. How fortunate that the invitations made no mention of an engagement. And now, good day to you."

He picked up his hat and departed.

Angela glared after his retreating back, her fury abating only when she heard his phaeton moving away in the street.

He was gone. The man she loved had not, in the end, loved her. She'd been only a convenience, and he had cast her off without a second thought.

Angela sank onto the sofa, a heavy weight settling on her chest. The ball. They couldn't call it off now without revealing the truth. They'd have to go ahead with it, pretending there had never been any motive but to entertain their friends. She would have to smile and dance and chat, aware that a hundred eyes scrutinized her for any sign of heartache. Worse yet, Lady Mary couldn't afford the expense, and Angela suspected her mother planned to sell the few jewels that remained to her to pay the costs.

Why had Meg engaged in such a mad business? Why, oh why had she written about it to Helen?

But that wasn't the heart of the problem, Angela knew. It was Edward. He cared nothing for her, nor ever had. Perhaps it was better to suffer this way now than to spend a lifetime yearning for the love he would never offer. Now if only she could persuade her heart to agree with her reasoning!

A carriage halted in the street outside. Hastily Angela dabbed a kerchief to her eyes, wishing her mother were home, but Lady Mary had gone calling and wouldn't be back for hours. She would have to keep up a front as best she could.

Sir Manfred was pleased when he entered to find Angela alone. She should not have entertained a gentleman in this fashion, but she clearly hadn't given the matter any thought. No doubt their frequent rides together had led to this increased intimacy, and it suited his purpose well.

"My dearest Angela." He swept across the room and took her hands in his. "How well you are looking." Although in fact she appeared a trifle strained.

"Thank you." She gestured to the sofa. "Would you care for some refreshment?"

He was on the point of saying he would like a drop of brandy when he recalled that a glass might prove a handicap. "No, no, not necessary, my dear."

They took their seats politely. Seemingly recalled to herself, Angela gazed about nervously. "I . . . I think I should summon a maid. For appearances' sake."

"Of course, but first let me say how glad I am to hear that your dear sister is returning to London."

This conversational dodge effectively distracted her. "Yes, she arrives tomorrow."

"Then she'll be at the ball." Sir Manfred noted how the girl grew ashen and wondered whatever was the matter. He could scarcely ask her point-blank. "I never could understand that business at Almack's. Danced with her myself that night, and she behaved splendidly."

"Meg is always splendid," Angela agreed, perking up a bit.

Seeing where her weak point lay, Sir Manfred continued to praise the absent Meg and noted with gratification that there was no further mention of summoning a maid.

He estimated that another quarter of an hour would elapse before Cynthia arrived. He mustn't play his cards too soon.

"May I know the colour of your gown?" Meeting a puzzled look, he added, "For the ball. So that I might send flowers."

"Oh. It's yellow."

She made no mention of an engagement, he noticed. Why should it be kept a secret, if in fact it existed? Perhaps Cynthia was mistaken. But in any event, he had decided upon his course and planned to pursue it to the end.

"That should look splendid on you." Sir Manfred saw his chance to move nearer the young lady. "Are you aware that some colours flatter one's skin and others detract?"

This gave Angela pause. "Well, I don't suppose I had thought about it. Although I do observe that some ladies look their best in black or dark blue, and others look finest in pale tones."

"Precisely. Hold out your hand."

Before Angela could respond, Sir Manfred moved from the sofa to kneel beside her chair. He laid a fold of the girl's creamy muslin skirt across her hand, and, with a rapid motion, untied his snow-white cravat and laid it there as well.

"Sir Manfred!" the girl protested.

"I am merely proving a point," he said in a mildly offended tone. "Look here. See how your gown flatters your skin, whereas were you to wear stark white, it is quite another matter."

Angela stared at her hand in perplexity. "I...I'm not sure I see what you mean, sir."

"Hmm." He gazed rapidly around the room. A bedchamber would have offered more scope, but then, if he were alone with Angela in her bedchamber, no such stratagems would be necessary.

A light blue embroidery cloth lay not far off in a sewing basket, and beneath it he found a spool of dark blue thread.

"Now I shall demonstrate with these two shades," he said, returning to Angela's side. "Regard this."

He lifted the cornflower-blue cloth, so much like the shade of her eyes, and set it against the ivory skin. "Very pretty," Sir Manfred observed. "You should wear this frequently."

"I have several blue gowns," Angela confirmed, "but not dark ones. Does that truly not look well on me?"

He replaced the cloth with the spool of thread. "There, you see for yourself how it overpowers you."

"I had always thought young girls avoided dark hues because they were depressing to the spirits." Angela was clearly fascinated in spite of herself by these revelations. "But it's because they make one look a dowd."

"Nothing could make you look a dowd," corrected Sir Manfred. Damn, not time yet for his move. "Let's find some other colours."

"Oh, yes!" Angela looked—he thought how to describe it—relieved. Perhaps she had feared some other topic of conversation. The forthcoming ball? No time to plumb the matter. After a rapid calculation, Sir Manfred shrugged off his bottle-green jacket.

"Sir!" Angela made fluttering motions with her hands. "You mustn't do this! Your sleeve would have sufficed."

"What? Oh, what a ninnyhammer you must think me!" Sir Manfred feigned a laugh. "All the same, look at this shade against your hand. What do you think of it?"

"It's better than the dark blue but not nearly so flattering as the light," Angela declared.

Fortunately Sir Manfred's vest was of yellow, a hue they hadn't yet explored. "I promise not to disrobe further, Miss Angela. Merely place your arm next to my chest. Yes. Ah, that is an excellent tint. I can scarcely wait to see you in your ball gown!"

He knelt there next to her chair, holding her hand close to his heart. From the street came the sound of a carriage drawing to a halt.

Angela's eyes widened in alarm and she opened her mouth to protest. As she did so, Sir Manfred gave her hand a sharp tug and the girl lost her balance.

As he had intended, she fell upon him. Quickly he pressed his lips to hers, just as Lady Cynthia Darnet thrust ahead of the butler through the door.

"Oh!" the countess squealed, a touch melodramatically, in his opinion. "I never imagined . . . Well! I've never been so shocked in my life."

The unfortunate target of this outburst looked as if she might expire. Sir Manfred felt a wave of pity as he helped her to her feet. She was a taking little thing, and there was no proof she had abused his kindnesses. Why not use this opportunity to accomplish what he had hoped for?

"I assure you, Lady Darnet, matters were not as they seemed," he muttered.

"Were they not?" Cynthia was in full sail now. "I find Miss Linley unchaperoned in a closed room, lying upon the floor, and you, Sir Manfred, in a state of undress!"

He glanced down at Angela where she sagged on the sofa and caught a glimmer of tears threatening to overflow. "Surely you would never repeat such a tale," he declared protectively. "If there's any fault, it must be mine."

"Not repeat it?" Lady Darnet stared at him indignantly. "If a young lady chooses to behave in such a disgraceful manner, society should know the particulars! As for its being your fault, sir, when a lady entertains a gentleman without proper supervision, she cannot cry foul if he takes advantage of the situation."

Angela shook her head dazedly. "I shall go away." Her voice came out in a whisper. "Meg and I...we shall go back home...."

"Nonsense!" said Sir Manfred.

His cousin looked as though she would like to kick him. "The girl is right. A most sensible idea. The Linleys don't belong in London. Two scandals in one season!"

"There will be no scandal," he informed her, "because Miss Angela and I are going to be married."

In the stunned moment which followed, Angela saw the events of the day flash before her. Edward's fury, the end of their engagement, the necessity to give the ball even though it would further impoverish Lady Mary, Meg's arrival full of the hope of resuming her place in the ton.

There was only one way of saving the people she loved, and Angela took it.

"Yes," she told Lady Darnet, "Sir Manfred and I are betrothed."

CHAPTER SEVENTEEN

WHAT A TALENT SHE HAD for getting herself into the briars, Meg reflected as the Bryn carriage rattled through the outskirts of Manchester. Oh, she would be so glad to get home!

At least there was Angela's wedding to look forward to, and the end of their financial difficulties. Not that Lady Mary would expect Edward to fund her establishment, but it would remove Angela's expenses, and the Linleys would naturally spend considerable time each year visiting the Cockerells.

She wouldn't mind in the least! Meg thought, her spirits beginning to rise for the first time in a day and a half as she pictured Helen's beloved face. They had so much to discuss.

Her thoughts returned then to Lord Bryn, and the spurt of happy anticipation died within her. The marquis had avoided her the rest of Sunday afternoon and evening, and she'd taken a subdued supper in the nursery. The children were also down at heart, whimpering and asking who would take care of them.

Indeed, who? she wondered unhappily. Germaine was to marry Squire Roberts, and of course there was no governess at hand. That pathetic Myra wouldn't have been fit, in any case. Given to vapours! What would she have done when confronted with a mouse, or a ghost?

The idea brought a smile to her lips for an instant. Then it was replaced by the image of his lordship's visage that

morning, dark and glowering. What had happened to the
love he had professed?

He had come out to see her off this morning, along with
Germaine and the children, no doubt to stave off speculation. There was nothing in his cold indifference to indicate
she had been anything more to him than a governess for his
children.

So many words had hung unspoken in the air. Part of her
yearned to abandon propriety and run to him, cling to his
sleeve, beg his forgiveness. A more spirited part of her had
ached to give him a good shake. What kind of man would
condemn them both to a lifetime of unhappiness as punishment for an error in judgement?

If only he did not hold so low an opinion of the ton. Unfair as it might be, his anger at himself over the death of his
servant and at London society for its frivolity had all devolved upon Meg. By her own bumblings, she had inadvertently come to symbolize all that he loathed and deplored.
Could any mere woman overcome such condemnation?

Her thoughts broke off as the coach rattled into the inn-
yard and the coachman came round to hand Meg down.

Instinctively she reached for the lorgnette. She had offered, this morning, to return it, but Andrew—no, Lord
Bryn, she must henceforth always think of him that way—
had waved her aside in annoyance.

The courtyard looked entirely different now, no longer
blurry and confusing but full of gesticulating people, bright
carriages, and scampering puppies. In some other mood,
Meg might have enjoyed watching the activity. Now the details contrived to remind her painfully of his lordship—the
arrogant turn of a gentleman's head, the soft happiness in
a lady's eyes so like her own but a few days past, the shouts
of children.

Turning away, Meg proceeded to make arrangements for
a seat on the mail back to London. If fellow passengers fa-

voured her with bold stares for travelling alone, she was not disturbed. The uncertain, easily cowed girl who had left London a few weeks before was gone forever.

So Meg returned to London, and to the shocking news that Angela was engaged to marry the wrong man. It was worse even than her own predicament, for Angela's happiness was far more important to Meg than her own.

"You can't mean to go through with it!" she cried as they sat in Lady Mary's private parlour on her first evening home, trying to absorb the rapid sequence of events which had taken place shortly before her arrival.

"I can and I shall," Angela said quietly. "Edward has no affection for me—of that I feel quite certain. One of us must marry soon, and Sir Manfred is an eligible specimen."

An eligible specimen! What chill words from the sister who a few weeks ago had been the most innocent and trusting of creatures. Meg turned to their mother. "You can't mean to let her. Surely you see it will ruin her life!"

"I see nothing of the kind." Lady Mary continued working at her embroidery, as if ordering the neat overlay of threads could untangle the web of their lives. "From what you've told us there's no hope of a marriage with Lord Bryn, nor from what I can see is there any chance of Edward's changing his mind. He can be infuriatingly pompous, although I'd not have said so were he my son-in-law."

"But Sir Manfred!" Meg protested, remembering the drunken gentleman who had abandoned her on the dance floor at Almack's. That larded, foppish fool must never touch her sister! "I'd sooner marry him myself, if someone must."

"I scarcely think we can hand Sir Manfred about like a prize horse." Angela produced the first genuine smile Meg had seen since her return to London.

"But you love Mr. Cockerell!"

"And you love Lord Bryn," responded her sister. "Since neither of us can have what we want, we must take what we can get."

"Most sensible," said Lady Mary.

Meg clamped shut her lips. In her weeks away from home, she had dwelt in her mind upon her family's endearing traits. She'd forgotten her mother's narrow practical streak and her sister's stubbornness.

What was she doing, thinking ill of the two people she loved most? It was because of her that they'd come to this pass!

"I'm terribly sorry, for my misadventures and for writing about them to Helen," Meg said. "It never occurred to me she would show the letter to her brother."

"I can scarcely believe it myself." Angela pricked her finger on her embroidery and tossed it irritably aside. "What do you suppose she had in mind? When I suggested telling him of our financial straits earlier, she rejected the notion."

"Quite rightly, too," said their mother.

"Surely you don't advocate intentional deception!" Angela exclaimed.

"The world in general and the ton in particular are built upon intentional deception," responded Lady Mary, to the girls' amazement. "Aging widows disguise their wrinkles with powders and paints, young rakes borrow endlessly and live beyond their means, and our own Prince Regent seeks to hide his bulk by squeezing it beneath a corset."

"But you cannot mean that we should be dishonest," said Meg. "I behaved most shamefully in disguising myself as a governess, did I not?"

"Where does one cease keeping up appearances and begin to be dishonest?" This flight of philosophy by the usually prosaic Lady Mary left both her daughters speechless.

"Angela has a respectable dowry. The state of her family's finances is none of her fiancé's concern."

Mrs. Pickney, the housekeeper, made a noisy approach down the hallway and through the open door. "Miss Cockerell has come to call, and begs your forgiveness for the lateness of the hour, my lady."

"What! Come to visit after supper?" Lady Mary stared at the housekeeper in horror. "Unheard of!"

"Perhaps she means to apologize," Meg said hopefully.

"It's most improper! We're not at home to her."

"Nonsense, Mother." Angela spoke with a note of authority which her sister had never heard before. "She's had to wait to slip out until Edward went to his club. You don't imagine he'd let her come calling, free as you please, in the middle of the afternoon!"

Grudgingly, their mother conceded the point and instructed the housekeeper to show their guest inside. Helen ran up the steps in a most unladylike manner, and arrived at the parlour breathless, her hair askew. "Meg! Welcome back!"

Without hesitation, Meg ran to her friend and embraced her. "How good you look! Have you had to sneak out?"

"I'm afraid so." Helen greeted Lady Mary and Angela. "I had to see you—to explain about the letter and see what I can do to patch things up."

"Nothing, I'm afraid." Meg joined their guest on the threadbare sofa. "My sister has managed to get herself promised to Sir Manfred, of all people!"

"It seems a logical solution," said Angela, but the tears glimmering in her eyes belied the surface calm.

"Logical! It's absurd. And so is my brother!" Had he stepped into the room at that moment, Helen left no doubt she would have assaulted him with any weapon at hand. "You can't go through with this, Angela, although I daresay even Sir Manfred is an improvement over Edward when it comes to good manners."

Mrs. Pickney carried in an armful of paper-wrapped packages. "Where would you like these, Miss Cockerell?"

"Oh, right here, thank you!" The girl jumped up and ran over. "These are some of my gowns for you, Meg, as you requested." She tore open the paper and pulled out masses of silk and lace and muslin. One bundle held matching ribbons, fans, gloves, and slippers.

"That's very kind of you, Helen," said Lady Mary, signalling the housekeeper to depart. "I fear we cannot accept such generosity."

"Oh, please!" The tall girl clasped her hands together. "It's the least I can do. Oh, Meg, I never meant to cause trouble for Angela. I had so looked forward to welcoming you both into the family. But the letter fell out of the book where I'd hidden it, and Edward chanced upon it. You can't know how horrified I was when I found it missing!"

Together, the three young women reviewed the events of the past few days from every angle, bringing the newcomer up to date on Meg's misfortunes and exploring at length Edward's reaction to the letter. At last Helen said, "We must make an attempt to set things right."

"Impossible," said Angela.

"For Meg, perhaps. Germaine would do whatever we asked, but I doubt she has much influence with his lordship," Helen said with a sigh. "However, my brother is another matter."

"You can't mean to say you believe he'd listen to you after all that has transpired!" Angela favoured their friend with a sceptical look.

"No, but I do believe he loves you, although he most likely doesn't even know it himself." Helen's face took on a determined grimness. "Surely he'd be seized by jealousy if he saw you in Sir Manfred's arms."

"Then he should have been the one who arrived instead of Lady Darnet. But I think not." Angela swallowed hard. "Helen, he would as soon be jealous of me as of... as of some milkmaid on your estates!"

"Don't set yourself too low, girl," said Lady Mary. "The man has eyes, and you're a fair sight for them."

"Very true." Helen reflected for a moment. "Unfortunately, he intends to remove to Somerset as soon as possible, taking the lot of us with him. I must find reason for him to stay."

Her listeners waited—Meg hopefully, Angela near tears, Lady Mary occupied in working loose a blue thread she had stitched in the wrong place.

"I have it!" Helen said at last. "I shall tell him we must attend the ball, to give the lie to rumours that he has broken off an engagement. Since my name and his are involved, he can hardly refuse."

"But won't you mention Sir Manfred?" asked Angela.

"Whatever for? Let Edward find out for himself."

"Helen, he'll banish you to Somerset until you're eighty!" declared Meg.

"Oh, even the stiffest boot softens with time." Helen shrugged. "I'll take the consequences, since it's my own carelessness which brought us to this pass. Now I'd best be off, before my absence draws too much attention. Aunt Emily won't betray us, but Rachel gabbles like a magpie." She kissed her friends on the cheeks and took her leave.

"Now there's a sensible girl," said Lady Mary after Helen had gone. "Takes matters into her own hands. We've left the running of the world to men, and you see what a packet of bad fish they've made of it. When it comes to matters of the heart, we'd best arrange things ourselves."

"But surely a young lady must wait for the gentleman to make the first move," said Meg.

"Not at all. She must merely make the gentleman think that he has made the first move." Her mother bit off a thread and laid aside her embroidery. "I think I shall retire. Tomorrow you must both help me prepare for the ball."

Meg and Angela retreated to their room in thoughtful silence. As a result of their mother's economies, there had been no replacement for Karen, so the two aided each other in undressing.

"What a pretty pass we've come to," sighed Meg, brushing out her sister's hair. "Both of us fallen in love, and neither of us loved in return."

"I cannot think Helen will meet with any success where Edward's concerned." Angela leaned her head back, as if it had become too heavy for her slender neck. "He has no feelings for me beyond disapproval. But at least his indifference when he learns of my engagement at the ball will convince even the most hardened gossip that there was never an attachment between us."

Meg kept her own counsel. She had never seen the pair together, but she suspected Edward's response would be infuriated jealousy. After all, how could anyone fail to love Angela?

After the candles were blown out, Meg lay awake for some time, wondering at the strangeness she felt in this familiar room. The soft rise and fall of Angela's breathing, while a pleasant reminder of her family's nearness, also underscored how far she was from Brynwood.

She would never see the marquis again. He had already written her off as a bad business and was probably casting about for a suitable wife. With his entrancing good looks, wealth and position, he was sure to find one soon.

Her heart clenched at the memory of his accusations. That he should think she was a mere prankster, come to make sport of him! How bitterly ironic, to be linked with the shallow creatures of fashion who'd sent Meg packing in the first place!

It was hopeless to love him, hopeless to lie here aching for the touch of his hand and the sound of his voice. She must put him from her mind and pray that in time her pain would dull.

Meg would have been deprived of even this small consolation had she known that, as of that very morning, Lord Bryn had set out for London.

CHAPTER EIGHTEEN

BRYN WAS NEVER afterward sure at precisely what point he decided to visit London for the first time in more than two years. Perhaps it was as he watched the carriage bear Miss Linley away, leaving him standing with clenched fists and an unfamiliar emptiness. Or perhaps it was when he was informed that the Geraints planned to remain in the neighbourhood for some weeks, pending Germaine's marriage to Squire Roberts. Naturally Andrew felt obligated to offer them the continuing use of his premises, although he found their presence a painful reminder of the past.

And then there were the downcast faces of the children, who were asking when Miss Linley was coming back and who was going to give them their lessons.

It was not as if he was afraid of going to town, he told himself, sipping an oddly tasteless glass of brandy in his study. There was no need to mix with the ton.

There was, indeed, a perfectly good reason that he should go. His man of affairs had erred badly in selecting the previous governess, since clearly the real Myra Lindsay had been unsuitable to deal with his wards. I shall go and select a governess myself, he decided firmly. Someone elderly—well, not so old she couldn't keep the children in hand, but definitely long in the tooth.

It was also true that from time to time he missed the comradeship of his friends at Brooks'. He recalled with amusement the witticisms they made at the expense of Beau Brummell and his foppish companions who frequented the bow window at White's and made audible comments about the passersby in Bond Street. What a pompous lot they were, and how he enjoyed skewering them with his chums.

There was one further matter with which he must deal. The defection of Miss Geraint had left the marquis in need of a wife.

Someone sweet and unassuming would suit him perfectly. A woman who would fade into the background, never laughing too loudly or dashing about the grounds yelling after the children—or taking his heart away and refusing to give it back.

Bryn searched his memory. Hadn't he heard that Lady Cynthia Darnet was widowed a year or so before? He remembered her vaguely as a quiet, elegant young woman. Perhaps she would suit.

Yes, the marquis would go to London the very next day and take matters in hand. And if that outrageous, unscrupulous Meg Linley had spread word of her prank, he would cut her down to the size of a turnip.

THE FOOD AT BROOKS' was passable, but only just. On Wednesday evening, the marquis consumed a dinner of boiled fowl with apple tart, chiding himself for forgetting the mediocrity of the club's cuisine.

Now where had all his friends gone these past few years? Unhappily Andrew searched the faces of those who passed by. Some he recognized, but they were elderly gentlemen of little interest to him.

An inquiry of the waiter produced the information that one fellow had married and retired to the country, another was serving with Wellington, a third had transferred his allegiance to the odious White's, and a fourth had been killed in a carriage accident. So it was with considerable relief, as he sipped his Madeira after dinner, that Lord Bryn espied Edward Cockerell.

The two had never been close, but they had belonged to the same set at Oxford. Andrew recalled some comment Miss Linley had made, that Edward had brought out her younger sister, and this gave him a moment's pause. But when Cockerell spotted him and approached, the marquis responded with a warm greeting.

"Glad to see you back in town." Edward took a seat in one of the wing chairs and signalled the waiter for a glass of sherry. "Business, old chap?"

"In a manner of speaking," said Andrew, adding frankly, "I've need of a governess for my wards, and while I'm about it, thought I'd take a look round for a wife."

Cockerell nodded agreeably. "Knew Germaine wasn't the right sort—too hoydenish," he said. "Was on the edge of getting leg-shackled to the wrong girl myself, but luckily I found out the truth about her in time."

The marquis listened in fascination to the story of Angela Linley. An artful deceiver, just like her sister!

When Edward came to the matter of Meg's letter, and Andrew realized his own affairs had been bruited about, he grew cold with anger. So the minx had boasted of her cleverness, despite her protestations of innocence!

With a sharp twinge, he saw that until this moment he had secretly cherished the hope that Miss Linley might yet prove to be merely a harmless eccentric who would magically reappear in his life and prove herself blameless. Now his last hope died. She must be punished. Oddly the prospect gave him no pleasure.

"As if that weren't bad enough, my sister rang a peal over my head when I tried to withdraw to the country," Edward was saying. "She insists we must make an appearance at the ball or the gossips will have a high time of it."

"Let them," muttered Lord Bryn. "Who gives a fig for their opinion?"

"Ah, but you must recall that I have an unmarried sister, and the family name to uphold." Mr. Cockerell assumed a prudish expression which, in Andrew's opinion, would have better fitted an old maid. "We haven't the protection of a title, you know."

Lord Bryn cut off a sharp retort. The fellow was right. Under the circumstances Andrew might even have attended the ball himself....

Attend the ball? Should he? Hmm. What a cork-brained notion. Or was it?

The idea rattled around in his brain. He hadn't yet fixed on a method of repaying Miss Linley for her betrayal, but this could be the perfect opportunity.

"I say." Andrew cleared his throat. "Perhaps I should come with you. Give me a chance to see these Linleys in their home setting. Can't deny I'm curious."

Edward sat up straighter, clearly pleased by the distinction of being singled out by the marquis. "Can't see any objection to that, old chap. Deuced affair's Friday night. We'll have supper at our house first—we lay a first-rate table."

"Delighted," said Andrew. "By the by, have you any notion whether Lady Cynthia Darnet is in want of a husband?"

Edward frowned. It had occurred to him, since he learned the truth about Angela, that he might resume his suit, but something had halted him. Perhaps it was the memory of the countess's bad temper at the garden party.

At any rate, he wouldn't mind giving her up, particularly not if it meant an opportunity to increase the marquis's social indebtedness to him, which might prove useful at some future time. "Believe she is. If you like, we could call there tomorrow afternoon."

"Splendid," said Andrew.

The following morning, he arranged for an advertisement to be placed in the newspapers seeking a governess. With luck, the business would be concluded by early the following week. Then, mindful that his country wardrobe was ill-suited to town, the marquis forced himself to go shopping in St. James's.

What painful memories came back to him as he ordered Hessian boots, snowy cravats, a high-crowned beaver hat, striped silk stockings, and other necessaries. In his younger days, it had been Harry who followed dutifully behind, arranging for packages to be delivered and, when asked, proffering expert opinions.

He would never have approved Lord Bryn's purchase of a blue coat, waistcoat, and knee breeches that had been made for another gentleman but never claimed. They fitted well enough and were of good material, however, and there wasn't enough time before the ball for the marquis to have new items made up.

He was not a vain man, but he could see that the elegant clothing suited him. Rough clothes and worn boots might be acceptable in the country, but it was a long-forgotten pleasure to see himself well turned out.

A pity Meg had never seen him this way. How her face would have glowed! With a rush of tactile memory, the marquis recalled how she'd melted into his arms that night when he'd proposed. He could still smell the sweetness of her hair, still feel the soft firmness of her body. Until he met her, women had seemed to Lord Bryn to be a vaguely necessary fact of life, owed one's politeness but not worth expending much thought over.

Meg. How forcefully she came back to him now, teasing the children out of their bad moods, carrying armfuls of flowers from the garden, bringing light into the old house and into his life.

She had enchanted him like some minx from a child's fairy story. Only at the last moment had he broken free of her spell. Why did he wish now that he had remained forever entranced?

Angrily the marquis forced himself, on returning home, to concentrate on preparing for the afternoon's visit to Lady Darnet. She, as he recalled, had been a proper wife, tractable and above reproach.

It was shortly after four o'clock when Mr. Cockerell's phaeton arrived and the two gentlemen set off for the widow's home. They found the countess entertaining an elderly duchess and her niece. Through the murmur of polite greetings and how-good-to-see-you-agains, the air hummed with their thoughts.

Lady Darnet: The Marquis of Bryn! Come back to London, and visiting me! But in company with Mr. Cockerell. Whatever can that mean? Well, Edward has had his chance, and no doubt he nurses a tendre for that simpering miss. I'd give my left eye to marry a marquis, and a young one at that!

Edward: She regards Bryn as if she were assessing the cattle at Newmarket. What a conniving wench she is, in spite of her fine looks and title. Why did I never see it before? But damn it, she *is* suitable, at least. Whereas Angela... Oh, dash Angela!

Bryn: Now here's the sort of woman I ought to marry. Polite, even if she does smile as if her teeth pain her. Tepid sort of fish, I suppose, but ain't that what a wife's supposed to be?

As she ushered her visitors to their seats and thankfully bade farewell to the duchess's party, it occurred to Cynthia that she had best watch her step. There was no telling what the marquis intended by this visit. Certainly it would not do to favour him too markedly; Edward, being rid of his onetime inamorata, might still prove a good prospect. She decided it best not to mention Angela's engagement to Sir Manfred. Why risk provoking Mr. Cockerell?

"Lord Bryn, I cannot tell you how honoured I am to be among the first to welcome you back to town." She adopted her sweetest tones as she offered the callers refreshments and sank gracefully onto a chair, without bothering to introduce her elderly, dozing companion.

"Thank you," he said. The man was even handsomer than she remembered, with his dark, brooding eyes and aristocratic face. But lacking in conversation.

"What brings you to town?" she chirped. "The balls, perhaps, or the Opera? They've rebuilt it, you know, and it's simply splendid."

"His lordship is here on business," said Edward. "I say, are you attending the Linleys' ball tomorrow night?"

"Oh, yes, indeed." Cynthia smiled brightly at both gentlemen, wishing Lord Bryn would exert himself a trifle more. "I'm told everyone will be there, though I can't imagine why."

"Truly?" The marquis fixed her with a puzzled look. "Why should they not?"

The countess loved to gossip, particularly about people she didn't like. "I daresay you've missed the uproar earlier this season, that nodcock Miss Linley snubbing Beau Brummell and then claiming she didn't see him."

Bryn merely grunted. She took this as encouragement.

"And then Edward was kind enough to sponsor the sister, but she's a milk-and-water sort of miss and not worthy of him," Lady Darnet rattled on. "Best of all, everyone knows they're down in the pocket. I've heard that Lady Mary was seen selling her emeralds to a jeweller in Clerkenwell. Can you imagine, financing a ball with one's last penny?"

Andrew was finding this conversation singularly distasteful. He had endeavoured, since the previous evening, to harden his heart against Meg Linley, a task made more difficult by the information that her family was in financial straits. Perhaps she *would* be forced into the role of a governess, after all, and then some other man might find himself falling in love with the sprite who brought magic to his household.

Moreover, he retained an intense dislike of frivolous tattle. Even now, men were fighting and dying on the Continent to protect the safety of self-satisfied windbags like Lady Darnet.

But perhaps he was being unfair. The lady had no doubt been raised to believe that drawing-room conversation must be kept light and general. She was only performing her obligations as a hostess.

Edward was also finding her chatter irritating. His initial rage over Angela's deception had faded, despite his best attempts to whip it up. He knew why the Linley family had incurred the ruinous expense of this entertainment, and couldn't suppress a twinge of guilt.

Cynthia wasn't entirely a fool, and she guessed that her comments about the Linleys had fallen upon less than sympathetic ears. Hastening to explain herself, she added, "Not that I take pleasure in someone else's misfortune, but I cannot bear pretence. Do they think to trick the rest of us by putting on a gala affair? Perhaps they think to lure some wealthy husband."

Both men looked displeased. In Edward's case, one could understand, but what about the marquis? Cynthia wracked her brain to think of some connection between Lord Bryn and the Linleys, but arrived at none.

When he spoke again, it was on another topic entirely. "How do you feel about life in the country, Lady Darnet?"

On the verge of blurting that she despised rustication, she paused. Could the marquis be referring to his own situation? She'd come close to ruining her chances!

"It would depend on who one's companions were, of course," she said, silently vowing that five minutes after marrying the man, she would insist on spending the season each year in London.

"A cautious reply," he said.

"It would be dishonest of me to pretend I've spent much time away from town." Cynthia dimpled coyly. "Therefore I can only judge from a house party or two, and on that basis, I must say that it is one's company which determines everything."

"You don't like to ride?"

The countess despised horses. "Of course one must ride, for how else can one show off one's riding costume?" She laughed, pleased at how well she'd avoided an outright lie.

When her visitors left a short time later, the widow congratulated herself on her cleverness and began planning her next step. She'd surmised that the two men would attend the Linleys' ball. Well, so would she, and in her exceedingly low-necked new gown, she would set Lord Bryn's head spinning as she whirled in his arms.

Whoever had invented the waltz must have had Cynthia Darnet in mind.

CHAPTER NINETEEN

WHEN EDWARD COCKERELL informed his sister at the breakfast table that Lord Bryn would be accompanying them that night, she immediately saw two possibilities.

The first was complete disaster. Between her brother and the marquis, Angela and Meg Linley would both be reduced to tears and humiliated in front of society.

The second possibility was a triumph of the first order. Love would somehow find a way and everyone would live happily ever after.

Helen advised Edward that if he created any trouble, she would personally tie him to the tail of a runaway horse.

"I have no intention of creating a disturbance," he snapped, highly offended. "May I point out that I am not the member of the family who has a talent for getting us into scrapes?"

Helen was on the point of retorting when Rachel trounced in, her wispy hair stuck atop her head in a disordered imitation of her elders' coiffures.

"Go right back upstairs and have Agnes brush out your hair," Helen commanded.

"But I'm tired of being treated as a child! I'm almost thirteen!"

"Don't pout, Rachel." Edward glared over the rim of his coffee cup. "Do as your cousin says."

"I'm going to ask Mama!" The child stomped back through the house.

"You see what an example you set for her?" Edward took advantage of the situation to point out. "Always insisting upon having your way. A woman should allow herself to be shaped by her guardian."

"Oh, indeed?" returned Helen. "I'm to bat my eyes and flirt like Lady Darnet, am I? A splendid example of the fair sex she is, that hypocritical schemer."

"Your language!" Her brother looked shocked.

"Never mind." She realized she'd wandered off on the wrong path. "I want your guarantee that neither you nor Lord Bryn will take any steps to embarrass Angela or Meg."

"One can hardly make such a vow on behalf of someone else, can one?" Edward snorted dismissively. "Particularly a marquis. You'd do better to try to engage his affections yourself, my dear. Two seasons and you haven't made a match."

"I have my share of admirers," said Helen, which was true. In fact, she'd refused two offers of marriage that same month, as her brother well knew. She preferred to enjoy her freedom as long as possible. "Well, you can tell Lord Bryn for me that if he harms either of my friends, I'll tie *him* to the tail of a runaway horse."

"I shall do no such thing." Her brother rose from the table and departed just as Aunt Emily entered with a much-abased Rachel and her gleeful younger brother, Teddy, in tow.

Helen spent the afternoon closeted with the emigré hairdresser, Pierre Lebeau, and was grateful for the excuse to avoid seeing Cynthia Darnet when she paid an unexpected visit.

The two women had never felt anything for each other beyond a mild dislike, but the countess refused to let that hinder her in any way. She had called upon Helen in the hopes of encountering Lord Bryn again and perhaps drawing from him in advance the request for a dance that evening. After all, he hadn't yet seen the current crop of unmarried girls, and Cynthia intended to do everything in her power to secure him for herself.

Standing in the hallway awaiting word whether Miss Cockerell was at home, Lady Darnet espied a young girl peeping at her from around a corner. She had no particular fondness for children, but the creature's open admiration stayed a sharp rebuff.

"I'm Rachel," said the girl. "You're Lady Darnet, aren't you?"

"So you just heard me inform the butler." In fairness, she had to admit the chit had excellent features and clear, youthful skin. In a few years she'd be the centre of attention, and Cynthia begrudged her every whit of it.

"I'd like to look like you." Unexpectedly, a sullen expression crossed the young face. "My cousins Edward and Helen are always telling me I'm too young. Why, this very morning—"

"Did Lord Bryn breakfast with you?" Lady Darnet dared to ask.

"Oh, no, but they were talking about him." Rachel scraped one toe along the parqueted floor. "They don't know that I read the letter."

"What letter?" This conversation was proving considerably more interesting than Cynthia had expected, and she glanced worriedly up the staircase for fear the butler would return too soon.

"The one Miss Linley wrote." Rachel could contain herself no longer. "What a lark that was! She pretended to be a governess and went to live with Lord Bryn, and when he found out, what a great fuss he made! Isn't that splendid? They'd simply die if they knew I'd read it!"

"Then we shan't tell anyone, shall we?" said Lady Darnet, and as soon as the butler conveyed Miss Cockerell's apologies, she went away quite satisfied.

What a worthwhile visit this had been! Precisely what use she would make of this information, Cynthia didn't yet know, but she had no doubt it would serve her well when the time came.

IT WAS with considerable misgivings that Helen set out that evening in the company of two gentleman, both of whom she could cheerfully have strangled.

Lord Bryn looked as devilish and dour as she had feared, and Edward wore the peevish expression of a young boy forced to attend the funeral of a disliked elderly relative. How two of the most beautiful and sweet-tempered women in the world could have fallen in love with this pair of coalhearts was more than Helen could fathom.

Angela was, at that moment, thinking much the same thing as she applied a light dusting of powder to remove the shine from her unblemished skin. She had felt both hope and distress upon learning the previous day that Edward would be attending. Surely he was only yielding to his sibling's insistence. The possibility of a reconciliation was, she knew, extremely small.

Angela had concentrated that week on the increasingly difficult task of exhibiting pleasantness toward Sir Manfred, who visited daily and showered her with damp kisses. Carefully she sidestepped his requests to set a date for the wedding, with the excuse that she could not think so far ahead until after the ball.

As for Meg, she had walked through the days like a person asleep. Obediently she ran errands to the florist's shop and the milliner's, supervised the placement of potted ferns and the arranging of candles, and purchased violet ribbons and Irish lace to retrim a lavender gown of Helen's.

All the while, she tried to grasp the enormity of the catastrophe which had descended upon them. Her own unhappiness was bearable; had she not previously resigned herself to an unmarried future? But she could scarcely bear to see her dear sister assume that look of passive acceptance whenever Sir Manfred came to call.

Briefly Meg wondered if she hadn't best set fire to his coat or otherwise offend him so grievously that he would stalk out of their lives. And so she might have done, in a fit of sisterly love, had it not been for the strain so apparent on Lady Mary's countenance.

The emeralds had been a family heirloom, passed down from her mother and grandmother. To sell them had meant to tear out a piece of her soul. Mary had prided herself since childhood on her ability to manage well, regardless of the circumstances. This talent had stood her in good stead after the death of her husband. Then had come the biggest decision of her life. Should she remain peacefully and solvently in Derby, or gamble her life's savings on her daughters' future?

She'd taken the risk, and had never regretted it until now. Despite her apparent indifference to Angela's feelings, Lady Mary was well aware that her daughter was making a woman's supreme sacrifice.

So she smiled upon Sir Manfred, who daily grew more odious in his patting and pawing of Angela, and ordered up an elegant midnight supper for the ball. Their guests, all unknowing, would be, in effect, consuming the Linleys' dreams.

The ballroom in their rented house was scarcely large enough for the purpose, but fortunately a mad crush was considered a sign of success, so Lady Mary didn't worry overmuch on that score. It was unfashionably located on the ground floor, but there was nothing to be done about that, either. Aired, dusted, and decked with flowers, it would have to do.

As was her custom, Lady Mary dressed in black on the occasion. The twilled sarcenet had served her for two seasons and, despite the snagged edges of the sleeves and hem, would have to suffice again tonight.

She smiled proudly at the sight of her two girls descending the staircase, Angela blonde and pale in light green crepe, Meg stunning and shadow-eyed in lavender silk.

"How splendid you look, both of you," Lady Mary exhorted. "Do try to appear a bit more cheerful. The season isn't over, Meg, and there's still a chance for you."

Her elder daughter nodded obediently and slipped an arm about Angela's waist. When their mother turned away, she whispered, "It's not too late. You needn't marry him."

"I must!" Angela murmured back. "Else we'll all land in debtors' prison before the year is out. And I told you how Lady Darnet found us."

Meg sniffed. "I never did like her. There's something havey-cavey about all this."

The sisters joined their mother in the entrance hall as the creak of carriage wheels and the jingle of harnesses sounded in the street outside. "Hold my hand when Edward comes in," Angela told Meg. "I mustn't show my feelings."

"Indeed not." Lady Mary's crisp tone proved remarkably steadying.

The arrivals began. There were Lord and Lady Sefton, the Drummond Burrells, Lady Jersey, the Cowpers, Lady Darnet in a shockingly low-cut gown, and, of course, Sir Manfred, who favoured his intended with a knowing wink.

Angela shifted uncomfortably, feeling hot beneath her gown. Perhaps Edward wouldn't come after all, she thought, and felt both relief and a sharp pang of dismay. For the first time, she truly entertained thoughts of what her future would be like.

How could she marry Sir Manfred? The touch of those clammy hands aroused her disgust, and the memory of his stolen kisses shuddered through her. Like most young women of her class, Angela had only the vaguest notion of what transpired between husband and wife. But she couldn't help being aware that it involved even more physical intimacy than she had yet experienced, and the notion filled her with horror.

Meg kept her head high, pretending not to notice the smirks and behind-the-hand remarks of some of the guests. Did they recognize the made-over gowns? Had they learned somehow of her escapade as a governess? Or was this merely the stale scandal left from Almack's?

Most of the whispering ended when Beau Brummell joined the throng, evidence that he harboured no ill-will. Meg, determined not to repeat her former mistakes, had prevailed upon her mother and won permission to wear the lorgnette dangling from a chain. Now she lifted it, peered at the Beau through the glass, and curtseyed prettily.

When she looked up, their eyes met and they shared a smile. There was one enemy won back, at least, she thought with a sigh.

As the press continued, Meg excused herself to see to the servants. She hurried into the ballroom, relieved to be free of the onerous duty of exchanging compliments with people she largely disliked. The wine and ratafia were flowing freely, and in the kitchen Meg found preparations well under way for the midnight supper. Their cook might lack the elegance of the French chefs employed by dukes and princes, but she was a dependable, down-to-earth sort who never panicked.

Under control, Meg thought, leaving the kitchen.

She paused, hearing the clatter of pans behind her and the tinkle of voices ahead. If only she dared make her escape! What a strain this evening was, a celebration of a tragic union. How gleefully the visitors drank and danced and laughed, who had only weeks before snubbed Lady Mary's family.

I have become too cynical for life in town, Meg reflected.
*One can only dine upon swans' tongues and French fruits
for a year or so, and then the palate becomes weary and one
longs for a bit of boiled chicken and fresh strawberries.*

In spite of herself, her thoughts went back to Brynwood.
How happy she had been there. How idyllic those few
weeks. Playing with the children, going on picnics ...

The memory of a pair of strong arms and gently insistent
lips overwhelmed her, and she quickened her step back toward the entrance hall.

As it happened, scarcely had Meg departed than the
Cockerell party made its appearance. Angela saw Helen first
and gave her a tremulous smile. Then came a tall gentleman whom she did not know, followed by Edward. Their
gazes met ever so briefly and then both looked away. Edward's expression was impatient, as if he longed to be done
with the evening.

And so he must, Angela thought, drawing herself up
straighter and recalling the announcement to be made later
that night. It would make no difference to Mr. Cockerell
whom she married, but at least her family would be safe.

"Good evening." Helen swooped forward to kiss the
cheeks of mother and daughter. "I hope you don't mind,
but Edward invited an old friend."

Lady Mary was staring at the tall man with a curious
expression, Angela noted. Who could he be?

"Meg isn't ill, is she?" Helen continued, leaving her two
escorts waiting to proffer their greetings.

"No, just gone to check on the preparations," said Angela, since her mother remained speechless. Whatever had
got into Lady Mary?

Thankfully, Angela caught sight of her sister approaching down the hallway, extending her hands to Helen. "How
good to see you!" Meg said. "You're looking splendid."

"So are you." Helen glanced at the gown meaningfully and winked.

Meg looked up at the men and turned as white as a come-out gown. "Lord Bryn," she whispered.

At once Angela understood her mother's reaction. She wished they had cancelled the ball, and to the devil with what society would say! Oh, Lord, how were they to survive this night?

CHAPTER TWENTY

IT WAS LADY MARY who recovered first, extending her hand to the marquis. "How delightful to see you back in London," she said. "We're honoured to have you as a guest."

"Charmed, madam," he replied, bowing politely over her hand.

Meg's initial pained reaction muted into disbelief touched with fear. Was it his intention to embarrass her at her own sister's engagement party? Surely he would not stoop so low, but what could account for his unexpected presence in London?

Her anxiety was in no way relieved when the marquis asked her for the first dance. She knew that stormy glint in his eyes too well to imagine that he had forgiven her transgressions.

"Why have you come?" she asked bluntly as he escorted her into the ballroom. There was no sign of tenderness in his touch, but her body swayed toward him of its own accord. Whatever bonds tied them together had not yet fully come undone.

Taking her question at its face, he said, "As you may recall, I have need of a governess. I thought to hire one in person this time, and one usually finds the best governesses in London."

"But why have you come to our ball?" Meg tried not to meet his eyes. She could not bear the coldness there, but neither could she look away.

Before replying, the marquis placed one hand on her waist, as required by the waltz, and pressed his palm against hers. As the music began, they set off together with a natural rhythm, each sensitive to the other's least motion. "Edward invited me, and I thought it might be amusing."

"Amusing?" Would he never cease this half-sneering tone? Was this truly anger, or a side of him she had merely failed to observe through blind infatuation?

Lord Bryn gave no sign of noticing her distress. "I was interested to learn that you spread word of your prank among your friends."

Meg could not stifle a gasp. "So that's why everyone was gossiping about me! But I told no one outside my family. Except my dearest bosom bow, of course."

"Indeed."

He could have given lessons to a block of ice. Justifiably, perhaps, she must concede. Being on such intimate terms with Helen, she had felt it only natural to confide in her, but she could well understand how different such an act must look to his lordship. Still, Helen would never have gossiped.

"It must have been Edward." Meg pressed her lips together grimly. "He read the letter I wrote to his sister, who is my closest friend. The information was meant for no other eyes than hers."

"Ah." Lord Bryn's countenance lost a bit of its superciliousness. "Perhaps I misunderstood. It was Edward who spoke to me of the matter, and I assumed you had intended it to be general knowledge."

"I certainly did not!" exclaimed Meg. "You came here to punish me, then?"

"It had entered my mind." The marquis looked almost, but not quite, ashamed of himself. "I care little for what others may say, but it is not in my nature to sit idly by while I am made a laughingstock."

"Well, you may return home to Brynwood assured that I have kept my word," Meg snapped. "I, my lord, have never behaved toward you in a mean-spirited fashion. Nor shall I in future, though you give me much provocation."

The music concluded at that fortuitous moment. Angrily she removed herself from his grasp and stalked away, leaving Lord Bryn standing dismayed in the centre of the floor.

Meg's fury surprised even her. She had felt shame, longing, sorrow, and the awareness of a deep abiding affection when she first saw the marquis this evening. But that he would come into the bosom of her family and seek to humiliate her was outside of enough!

Taking refuge in a bower of potted palms, she clenched her fists and forced her temper under control. She could not, must not disgrace herself this evening. No sooner had the heat of her anger abated than a cold misery took its place. The man she loved had purposely misinterpreted her every action. He sought only to blame and to get revenge. What possibility could there be for reconciliation now?

She must not cower here, giving fodder to idle tongues. As a hostess, she must smile and pretend merriment. Struggling to put on the false face required by society, Meg remembered that Angela's happiness lay in the balance tonight. In a few hours, the engagement would be announced and her sister's fate sealed.

Edward. If only he could be brought round somehow. Could he be made jealous?

Meg took three deep breaths, a trick her mother had taught her long ago for controlling the emotions. Yes, she must turn her attentions to the haughty Mr. Cockerell. It would distract her from her own sorrow, and perhaps show a way to win him back for Angela.

A survey of the room found Edward dancing indifferently with his sister, nodding to acquaintances and paying no attention to his former love. The very manner in which he ignored Angela bore mute testimony to his attachment to her, for only with deliberate intent could he have avoided her so completely.

Meg gazed about. Sir Manfred, wearing a self-satisfied expression, was swapping tales with an earl and a viscount. He clearly saw no need to woo his own fiancée at their engagement ball.

Courage, Meg counseled herself, and moved forward into the trio of men. Immediately the talk halted, and she gathered that the conversation had been risqué.

"May I speak with you a moment, Sir Manfred?" She smiled sweetly and drew him aside.

"Nothing wrong, I hope?" he said. Not a bad man, Meg reminded herself, but so lumpish. His hair had an oily glaze to it, and red veins showed in his eyes.

"Not precisely..." She forced herself to gaze earnestly into those puffy eyes. "It's my sister."

"Angela? What the devil! Not ill, is she?" The fellow bristled with concern. Had he not smelled so strongly of the brewery, Meg might have felt more sympathy.

"No, but—this is merely a suspicion of mine, nothing that she's said outright—I think she may be having second thoughts," Meg said. "The normal sort of thing among young girls. I think it best that you reassure her of your affections."

"Eh? Oh, right, right you are." Sir Manfred tossed back the last of his sherry, handed Meg the glass, and set out in search of his prey.

Forgive me, Angela, Meg begged silently. Stiffly, she turned to greet a party of latecomers, trying to ignore the painful sight of the marquis dancing with one of the season's Incomparables, a giddy girl whom Vanessa and Tom would have routed from the nursery inside of five minutes.

The thought of that gleeful pair brought a fleeting smile to Meg's lips. Oh, she did miss them! But she must attend to what an elderly dowager was saying or risk insulting her guests.

Across the room, Edward was finishing the dance with his sister. "How soon can we leave?" he murmured.

"Not for at least another half hour," she replied imperiously, and smacked him on the arm with her fan for emphasis.

Another partner claimed Helen, and left alone, Edward surveyed the room. He caught Lady Darnet's eyes upon him. Dash it, she looked splendid tonight in silver gauze over a blue underskirt, and never before had she exposed so much of her creamy bosom. On any other woman, the gown would have been brazen, but despite the décolletage, the countess still managed to resemble an ice sculpture.

Might as well dance with the woman, he told himself, starting across the room. No point the evening's being a complete waste. Unintentionally, his vision swept across the figure of Angela Linley talking to that fop Sir Manfred. Edward halted without realizing he'd done so. What the devil did that fat fool think he was doing, laying his arm about Angela's waist in such a familiar manner?

None of my concern, he told himself, and resumed his journey. With a modest curtsey, the countess agreed to join him in a gavotte.

Remembering Bryn's interest in the widow, Edward looked for his friend. Ah, there he was across the room, swirling a glass of wine and staring fixedly at Meg Linley as she darted to and fro exchanging pleasantries.

The opening strains of the music floated through the air, and Edward turned to the beaming countess. Bryn could jolly well straighten out his own life without anyone's help.

Now how had Sir Manfred and Angela come to join this set for the gavotte? Oh, yes, the chap was Lady Darnet's cousin. Damned annoying, these relationships and entanglements! thought Edward. The rotund fellow was making a cake of himself over the ashen-faced girl. Not that Mr. Cockerell cared in the least, but he did think the man might have the good breeding to refrain from publicly squeezing the chit's hand and whispering in her ear.

Edward performed the elaborate movements of the dance out of habit. He was thinking how sad and lost Angela looked. Why did she allow that Manfred chap to take such liberties? Instead of protesting when he patted her shoulder or fingered one of her curls, the girl merely lowered her eyes in resignation.

Someone ought to plant the cad a facer!

Lady Darnet was not oblivious to her partner's preoccupation. Edward was far more besotted with that simpering Angela than she had imagined. Well, the marquis presented a superior prospect, she decided, turning her attention to him as she wove through the dance.

The tall figure across the room stood aloof from the merriment, but there was no mistaking the way he took in every gesture Meg Linley made. How could he be so fascinated by a girl who had played a scandalous jest at his expense? the countess wondered. *I shall put him off her quick enough!* she resolved.

The gavotte ended. Sir Manfred tugged at Angela's hand and led her out into the garden. After a disbelieving stare, Mr. Cockerell followed. The countess, free to pursue her goal, made her way through the crowd to Lord Bryn.

A large purplish matron and a thin pinkish girl had the marquis half-surrounded, and from the facial expressions of the three Cynthia gathered that the women were seeking, and failing, to impress him with the chit's attractions.

"My lord, how pleasant to see you so soon after you called on me," she said, letting her words drop like a blanket across the conversation.

"Ah. Lady Darnet." As she had hoped, the marquis disengaged himself and asked her to dance.

Yet another of her wishes was granted. The dance proved to be a waltz.

"London has sorely missed your presence," she said in her most cultivated tones as they whirled about the room together. He danced correctly but stiffly, as if partnering a broomstick.

"I find that difficult to credit." The marquis's lip curled. "The ton is an animal which, unlike the fox or hare, can replace a missing limb without any but the most superficial discomfort."

"Perhaps I should have phrased my statement differently." Though mildly vexed, Lady Darnet was determined to retain her composure. "I meant that I have thought of you from time to time and wondered how you were."

To the best of the marquis's recollection, he and the countess had known each other only slightly at best before her marriage and before he succeeded to his title. On the other hand, why should he cavil at her compliments? Hadn't he been considering only the day before taking her as a wife? True, she was blatantly shallow, but so, he told himself, was every woman.

The countess leaned closer, enticingly, although her natural coldness precluded any physical response on the part of the marquis. "Did you notice that gown Meg Linley is wearing?" she confided. "It formerly belonged to Helen Cockerell."

"Did it indeed?" The marquis recalled his companion's remarks of the previous day about the Linleys' lack of funds. Why should Lady Darnet think it concerned him?

"They say the Linley girl is hanging out for a rich husband," Cynthia invented artfully. She had his full attention now! "Likely to take the first man she can bring up to snuff, or so they say." At that moment Meg was chatting with an elderly baron, and the countess nodded meaningfully.

Bryn stared at the pair with distaste. Surely his Meg wouldn't leg-shackle herself to an old wrinkle-face merely to obtain money!

Lady Darnet persisted. "Lady Mary will have scarcely a feather left to fly with after this ball, shabby as it is. Plans to sell off her daughters, I've no doubt."

The words freckled across the complexion of Lord Bryn's thoughts. Meg, forced into a marriage of convenience? That was certainly a different matter than trading oneself off willingly.

Could his own wealth have accounted for her conduct at Brynwood? he wondered. Unbidden, an image sprang to mind of her imploring face as she declared her love for him. She must be a good actress to have played the role of heartbroken maiden so convincingly. Yet she hadn't hesitated to rip up at him this evening when she learned of his ignoble intentions. Was that the conduct of a chit seeking a wealthy match? The girl was certainly a puzzle.

The marquis felt a surge of relief when it was time to relinquish Lady Darnet to another gentleman. Her malicious chitchat had become sorely trying.

The countess watched him go, her face pinched with sour disappointment. Why hadn't her ruse worked? He was observing Meg Linley as closely as ever! Well, she would put a stop to that when the time came. And to Edward's infatuation with the sister, as well!

In the garden certain matters were taking place that would have fascinated Meg and discomfited Cynthia, had either been present to observe. The scene might have come from a melodrama at Covent Garden. Or perhaps a farce.

Enter Sir Manfred and Angela. Cross to shadowed arbour, where the gentleman attempts to press his mouth to the lady's and she is seized by involuntary shudders. Enter a second gentleman, who dashes across to the couple and shouts, "Unhand her, you cad!"

Sir Manfred steps back in astonishment, but the fury of his opponent drives him reluctantly back toward the house....

"You don't understand." Angela gazed upward through her tears as Edward stood glowering over her. "I'm supposed to marry him. He came to call one day while I was alone. He knocked me to the floor just as his cousin came in and caught us compromised. Besides, there's Mother—"

"Hang it all, Angela, you can't marry that windbag!" Edward caught her in his arms and pressed her trembling form against him. "If you have to marry someone, then I guess it might as well be me."

With her faint remaining strength, Angela pulled free. "I can't, Edward. I love you so much. How can I accept a loveless marriage, always longing for the affection you can't give me? I'd be better off with Sir Manfred." She began to weep in earnest.

"A loveless marriage?" In a rare moment of insight, the truth about his own heart penetrated Edward Cockerell's stiff-necked pride. "But I adore you, my sweet. It was only... my duty... that is, how could I grant my own happiness, at the expense of my... What the devil am I talking about?"

He dropped to one knee, and this time felt no embarrassment about pressing his suit with ardent words which astonished both him and his listener. Nearly afloat with joy, Angela agreed to resume their engagement.

As for Sir Manfred, he was not by nature a coward, any more than any other gentleman who has always lived comfortably off inherited money and devoted himself to his own pleasures.

He had relinquished Angela not from fear of injury—although he had a healthy respect for Edward Cockerell's fists—but from a knowledge of his own guilt. It was he who had broken the loving couple apart, he believed, with his stratagem of trapping the young lady into an engagement. Therefore he could scarcely contend he'd been wronged, or had the prior claim. Well, Sir Manfred would show the pair that he suffered from no pangs of unrequited love.

Inside the ballroom, his gaze fell upon Meg Linley standing beside her mother. With a bow, he requested her company and was granted it. The lively country dance was followed by yet another waltz and, with reckless disregard for propriety, Sir Manfred insisted upon two dances in a row.

"Going to be family and all," he muttered, taking advantage of the sister's ignorance to demonstrate his heart-wholeness to Angela, who had reentered the room on Edward's arm.

As he had been following Meg's movements throughout the evening, the marquis did not fail to observe Sir Manfred's breach of etiquette. Nor did his response differ significantly from that of Edward, when the latter viewed the same gentleman with Angela a quarter of an hour earlier.

What was wrong with the girl? the marquis demanded silently. Meg couldn't actually intend to marry that fop for his money, could she?

Lord Bryn had only a slight acquaintance with Sir Manfred, but he did recall that the gentleman was comfortably fixed. Not a great catch, but an adequate one in view of the Linleys' difficulties.

His heart turned over at the sight of Meg smiling tensely up at the portly fellow, as if forcing herself to be polite. He naturally failed to connect her conduct with the fact that she had just sighted her sister and Edward Cockerell entering the room together. Certainly he had no inkling that Meg was trying to prevent a nasty scene by soothing Sir Manfred's presumed ill-temper.

It was at that moment that Cynthia, making one last attempt at reviving her chances of becoming a marchioness, strolled by and murmured, "Do you expect them to make the announcement this very evening?"

Far from arousing the marquis's disdain, her words had the opposite effect. Andrew saw of a sudden that he loved Meg desperately and that to the best of his knowledge she loved him. The only thing standing in their way was his own damnable pride.

The same pride had led him to ignore his trusted Harry that tragic day on the Peninsula, with results which would haunt the marquis as long as he lived. He was making the same mistake again, but in such a different form that he had almost failed to recognize it. He had allowed himself to wallow in self-righteousness without a thought for Meg's future.

Her marriage to that unpleasant excuse for a man would be, in its own way, a death of all which was happy and free in her soul. She had told Bryn herself that the reason she perpetuated the hoax at Brynwood was because she loved him. Yet he had gone on brooding and doubting her motives until it was almost too late.

He saw in that moment what it would mean to him if he continued this show of indifference. The future stretched ahead, a long empty staircase of years, without Meg to brighten his household. There would be endless breakfasts with some tedious woman pouring coffee and gossip across the table from him, endless evenings filled with polite phrases and reproaches at his coldness, endless nights of tossing and aching for the scent of her hair across his pillow. He must take action now, or the war was lost. Without another hesitation, the marquis strode across the room.

Sir Manfred felt a hand clamp on to his shoulder. He looked up to see a dark glowering face and hear a voice commanding him to relinquish Miss Linley. Who would have suspected Lord Bryn would snarl at him in this manner over a girl of no importance? Dash it, things simply weren't going his way this evening! Why had he ever thought he wanted to give up his bachelorhood?

Lady Darnet watched in fury as the marquis replaced her cousin in Meg Linley's arms and waltzed her out into the garden. Her anger fanned into flame as she noted Edward Cockerell and a glowing Angela speaking privately with Lady Mary.

She would have the last word yet! Barely controlling her fury, the countess grabbed her luckless cousin and sent him scurrying for a glass of sherry. Oh, how she hated to waste even a moment, but she must bide her time.

Meanwhile, snatched without warning from the dance and marched out-of-doors, Meg had no inkling that Lord Bryn meant her anything but further reproach. Well, she would not wait for him to strike first!

"Have you uncovered some other imaginary scheme of mine?" she demanded when they were alone in the garden. "Have two more ruffians come to call for their cousin, who is not me?"

"Prickly lass," said the marquis.

Meg glared at him. "This may be sport to you, my lord, but I have serious matters to attend to." Even now, Sir Manfred might be raising hue and cry over Angela's defection.

"So I observed."

"What do you mean?" She folded her arms, expecting some new insult.

"Lady Darnet informs me that you are forced to marry for money," said the marquis gently, adding in an unconscious paraphrase of Edward's words to Angela, "If you must do so, then I am considerably richer than Sir Manfred."

"Is that meant to be a proposal?" Meg couldn't believe it. Was the man mocking her? How cruel, when he must know that she loved him! Well, she had thrown herself at his feet once and would not do so again. "Hardly romantic."

"Shall I go down on one knee?" His handsome mouth twisted wryly. "It's a bit damp for that this evening, wouldn't you say?"

How appealing he could be when he smiled! Some other time, under some other circumstance, she might have laughed and touched that curving cheek. But now she must disabuse him of this nonsense about a forced marriage. "Well, you're quite safe, because I have no intention of marrying Sir Manfred or anyone else. So you needn't sacrifice yourself."

"Dash it, Meg, I love you!" The words burst out of Lord Bryn before he could stop them. "It's taken me a while to see it, that's all, and I don't mean to waste time begging for dances and rides in Hyde Park. Just say yes and be done with it."

She slanted a dubious look up at him. "You really want to marry me?"

"I've just said so." He was feeling somewhat truculent at the cavalier manner in which she treated his suit. "I need a wife, and you'll do as well as any. Dammit, that's not what I mean. I need you. The children need you. The house needs you. If you don't marry me, I'll carry you off to Scotland and force the matter. Is that clear?"

"Perfectly," she said. "You leave me no choice. I shall have to marry you."

It took a moment for the import to hit home. "You're saying yes?"

"I am." Didn't he know she cared nothing for flowery courtships, that all she wanted was to be alone with him once more as they had been that night when she learned what it meant to love as a woman?

"Not just because I, er, threatened you?"

"Actually," Meg said, laughter bubbling from her lips, "I was thinking of hauling you off to Scotland myself. But it might look odd to the children."

He uttered a shout and gathered her in his arms.

The music was quite soft, and more than one set of ears in the ballroom heard that joyous cry. The pair which mattered belonged to a spiteful, determined young countess.

When, half an hour later, Lady Mary silenced the orchestra and stepped onto the platform to make an announcement, Lady Darnet was ready. "I am happy to tell you that both of my daughters are engaged to be married," said the hostess, waiting while a collective gasp rose from her audience. "My elder daughter, Margaret, shall marry Lord Bryn, Marquis of Brynwood, and my younger daughter, Angela, is betrothed to Mr. Edward Cockerell."

Before the crowd could recover from its astonishment, Lady Darnet raised her voice, her courage bolstered by repeated glasses of sherry. "This is an outrage!"

Heads swiveled. Eyelids blinked. Silence rippled across the room.

"Meg Linley disguised herself as a governess and invaded Lord Bryn's home, living with him in the most scandalous manner until he tossed her out!" the countess shouted, her voice cracking slightly on the last word.

No one moved, the listeners being too shocked to respond.

It was Helen Cockerell who spoke first. "Nonsense! It's true that Miss Linley visited Lord Bryn, but she was in the company of my cousin, Germaine Geraint, who I'm sure will attest to the propriety of their conduct."

This countermove Cynthia had not foreseen. Blast the girl! Well, there was still that odious Angela left to cut down to size.

"As for the younger sister, I myself witnessed her sprawled on the floor with Sir Manfred in a state of undress," she declared.

The murmur which greeted this sally was not entirely friendly. It might even have been described as openly sceptical.

To the countess's horror, her cousin himself refuted this testimony. "Stuff and nonsense! I merely walked into the room, slipped and knocked Miss Angela to the floor. My own clumsy fault. Cynthia, you've got yourself foxed again on sherry, and I'll not have it!"

With this juicy disclosure of her allegedly drunken habits, he grasped Lady Darnet by the elbow and removed her bodily from the room. "Had enough of this folderol," he muttered as he retrieved their cloaks from a servant. "There's only so much a man can take and no more."

Overcome by rage, the countess cursed him with phrases colourfully descriptive, and seldom if ever heard in a respectable home. By the time the feuding pair had departed, it was clear that many a door would be closed to Lady Darnet for months to come.

As for Lady Mary, she regretted this unfortunate interruption, but nothing could dim her happiness at supper as she watched Angela teasingly feed Edward a morsel of crab cake and Meg rest her head against the marquis's shoulder, both of their faces a study in contentment.

For a bit of fluff and a chit who couldn't see, they hadn't done half badly, thought Lady Mary, and helped herself to a celebratory glass of claret.

Harlequin Regency Romance™

COMING NEXT MONTH

#15 THE VIRGIN'S HEART by Coral Hoyle

Amidst the backdrop of country courting and competition, Alexander Monk is determined to win back Roxanne Costain, the woman who had ended their betrothal four years before. A treasure hunt, conceived to make them "partners," begins as a romp but ends in treachery and near tragedy for Roxanne and Alex. The brush with disaster seals their love and they pledge anew their vows to wed.

#16 MEN WERE DECEIVERS EVER by Gwyneth Moore

When Helena Hammond learns her fiancé was killed in the war, she accepts the proposal of marriage made by Lt. Peter Clivedon. Her family is deeply in debt— she sees no alternative. Once married and removed to Whisperwood, Helena grows very fond of Peter. But the idyllic interlude is shattered when Helena learns Peter tricked and deceived her into marriage. Though she leaves Whisperwood vowing never to come back, Peter can only hope she never finds out the devastating truth behind his proposal.

Especially for you,
Christmas from
HARLEQUIN HISTORICALS

An enchanting collection of three Christmas
stories by some of your favorite authors captures
the spirit of the season in the 1800s

TUMBLEWEED CHRISTMAS by Kristin James

A "Bah, humbug" Texas rancher meets his match in his
new housekeeper, a woman determined to bring the spirit
of a Tumbleweed Christmas into his life—and love into
his heart.

A CINDERELLA CHRISTMAS by Lucy Elliot

The perfect granddaughter, sister and aunt, Mary Hillyer
seemed destined for spinsterhood until Jack Gates arrived
to discover a woman with dreams and passions that were
meant to be shared during a Cinderella Christmas.

HOME FOR CHRISTMAS
by Heather Graham Pozzessere

The magic of the season brings peace Home For
Christmas when a Yankee captain and a Southern heiress
fall in love during the Civil War.

Look for HARLEQUIN HISTORICALS CHRISTMAS
STORIES in November wherever Harlequin books are sold.

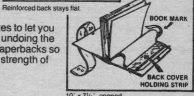

HARLEQUIN'S "BIG WIN"
SWEEPSTAKES RULES & REGULATIONS
NO PURCHASE NECESSARY TO ENTER OR RECEIVE A PRIZE

1 To enter and join the Harlequin Reader Service, scratch off the pink metallic strips on all your BIG WIN tickets #1–#6. This will reveal the values for each sweepstakes entry number, the number of free books you will receive and your free bonus gift as part of our Reader Service. If you do not wish to take advantage of our introduction to the Harlequin Reader Service but wish to enter the Sweepstakes only, scratch off the pink metallic strips on your BIG WIN tickets #1–#4 only. To enter, return your entire sheet of tickets intact. Incomplete and/or inaccurate entries are not eligible for that section or section(s) of prizes. Not responsible for mutilated or unreadable entries or inadvertent printing errors. Mechanically reproduced entries are null and void. Be sure to also qualify for the Bonus Sweepstakes. See Rule #3 on how to enter.

2. Either way your unique Sweepstakes numbers will be compared against the list of winning numbers generated at random by the computer. In the event that all prizes are not claimed, random drawings will be held from all entries received from all presentations to award all unclaimed prizes. All cash prizes are payable in U.S. funds. This is in addition to any free, surprise or mystery gifts that might be offered. The following prizes are awarded in this sweepstakes: *Grand Prize (1) $1,000,000; First Prize (1) $35,000; Second Prize (1) $10,000; Third Prize (3) $5,000; Fourth Prize (10) $1,000; Fifth Prize (25) $500; Sixth Prize (5000)$5.

   *This Sweepstakes contains a Grand Prize offering of a $1,000,000 annuity. Winner may elect to receive $25,000 a year for 40 years without interest totalling $1,000,000 or $350,000 in one cash payment. Entrants may cancel Reader Service at any time without cost or obligation to buy (see details in center insert card).

3. Extra Bonus Prize: This presentation offers two extra bonus prizes valued at $30,000 each to be awarded in a random drawing from all entries received.

4. Versions of this Sweepstakes with different graphics will be offered in other mailings or at retail outlets by Torstar Corp. and its affiliates. This promotion is being conducted under the supervision of Marden-Kane, Inc., an independent judging organization. By entering this Sweepstakes, each entrant accepts and agrees to be bound by these rules and the decisions of the judges, which shall be final and binding. Odds of winning in the random drawing are dependent upon the total number of entries received. Taxes, if any, are the sole responsibility of the winners. Prizes are non-transferable. All entries must be received by March 31, 1990. The drawing will take place on or about April 30, 1990 at the offices of Marden-Kane, Inc., Lake Success, NY.

5. This offer is open to residents of the U.S., the United Kingdom and Canada, 18 years or older except employees of Torstar Corp., its affiliates, subsidiaries, Marden-Kane, Inc. and all other agencies and persons connected with conducting this Sweepstakes. All Federal, State and local laws apply. Void wherever prohibited or restricted by law.

6. Winners will be notified by mail and may be required to execute an affidavit of eligibility and release that must be returned within 14 days after notification. Canadian winners will be required to answer a skill-testing question. Winners consent to the use of their name, photograph and/or likeness for advertising and publicity in conjunction with this and similar promotions without additional compensation.

7 For a list of our most current major prize winners, send a stamped, self-addressed envelope to: WINNERS LIST c/o MARDEN-KANE, INC., P.O. BOX 701, SAYREVILLE, NJ 08871.

If Sweepstakes entry form is missing, please print your name and address on a 3″ × 5″ piece of plain paper and send to:

In the U.S.	In Canada
Harlequin's "BIG WIN" Sweepstakes	Harlequin's "BIG WIN" Sweepstakes
901 Fuhrmann Blvd.	P.O. Box 609
Box 1867	Fort Erie, Ontario
Buffalo, NY 14269-1867	L2A 5X3

Wonderful, luxurious gifts can be yours with proofs-of-purchase from any specially marked "Indulge A Little" Harlequin or Silhouette book with the Offer Certificate properly completed, plus a check or money order (do not send cash) to cover postage and handling payable to Harlequin/Silhouette "Indulge A Little, Give A Lot" Offer. We will send you the specified gift.

Mail-in-Offer

OFFER CERTIFICATE

Item:	A. Collector's Doll	B. Soaps in a Basket	C. Potpourri Sachet	D. Scented Hangers
# of Proofs-of -Purchase	18	12	6	4
Postage & Handling	$3.25	$2.75	$2.25	$2.00
Check One				

Name _____

Address _____ Apt. # _____

City _____ State _____ Zip _____

ONE PROOF OF PURCHASE

To collect your free gift by mail you must include the necessary number of proofs-of-purchase plus postage and handling with offer certificate.

HRG-2

Harlequin®/Silhouette®

Mail this certificate, designated number of proofs-of-purchase and check or money order for postage and handling to:

INDULGE A LITTLE
P.O. Box 9055
Buffalo, N.Y. 14269-9055